Counter-Melody

Ryan DeRome

ISBN-10: 0692748989
ISBN-13: 978-0692748985

DEDICATION

To LJR

CHAPTER 1

Discarded and faded, a single candy wrapper tumbled by Alex as he waited for the city bus to arrive. It had been a somewhat long and arduous day at work and he was more than ready to relax for the rest of the evening as he patiently stood and soaked up the late afternoon sun. His hands were sore from pushing the broom and his cleaning cart from room to room and from exhibit to exhibit, his length of employment had been so far very brief at the museum and he was reminded of what one of his new fellow coworkers said to him, "That cramping should go away in time."

Alex also realized that the next phase after the cramping would be calluses and it would be as if he wore a calling card as to his livelihood being that of physical laborer. He then closed his eyes and turned his head upward towards the sky to try and use the bright day as some sort of natural cure for what ailed him. It was the type of day that one longed for after the harsh winter in Chicago, the temperature was sixty-five degrees and the wind only slightly coaxed ones hair from one direction to another. Soon he felt the weather would be more favorable for riding his bike to work instead of relying on public transportation or begging a ride from a friend. Although the ride would be longer than what he was used to he enjoyed the thought having the freedom to travel at will and to take in the scenery.

There was a small crowd of strangers congregating several feet away while waiting for the bus to pick them up and he listened to the various conversations taking place as some people clearly knew each other and others did not but still spoke to pass the time. To Alex it was a comfort and commentary on mankind that total strangers could still harbor some welcoming feelings towards each other even in this large city. But still he felt very much on the outside standing in his blue jeans and trusty dark green windbreaker that always seemed to stay with him through thick and thin.

He had great difficulty admitting it but he had felt like

an outsider for quite a while and knew that it didn't always used to be this way. The hair on his head had not been washed since the day before and he tried to pin his apprehensive behavior towards others on the simplest of physical appearance flaws as several brief waves of pain shot through his stomach and chest. Not a single soul had a tan, but he knew his lack of color was from more than just avoiding the sun; Alex would even appear sickly pail in August. Or maybe it was the sweat that was gathering on his forehead on this perfect spring day and how nobody else would be showing such duress in these temperatures. All Alex could think of was whether or not his friend Robbie had made a successful purchase and how much he needed what they commonly referred to as 'the product' when they spoke in code.

The longing had grown over the past year from a fun fling enjoyed on occasions into a monster that controlled every motivation during his waking hours and even sometimes appeared as a specter in his dreams. His hands although cramped had become tightly balled into fists and his breathing became deeper and in a more rapid succession than an hour before. Alex worried that this would draw attention to him from this seemingly innocent crowd of strangers and they would pass their own brand of judgment on him. That thought scared him into a twenty-foot retreat as he reached for his phone to contact the friend in question.

"Alex buddy! What's shaking?" asked Robbie on the other end of the line. Alex struggled for composure as he was on the verge of begging for Robbie to come pick him up and to bring what he needed. "Well, just waiting for the bus that seems like it'll never fucking come", replied Alex knowing his poker face was not working nor would it ever in times like these. Robbie could also sense by the tone in his voice that Alex was in need of a fix and had made a cruel practice of toying with the man in his weaker moments. Robbie was going to be getting off of his shift at the warehouse within twenty minutes and knew his supervisor wouldn't approve of him talking on his cell phone during work, but he weighed that risk against the angst of Alex. "Are you still getting off at four forty-five today?" ask Alex already knowing the work schedule of his friend but still longing to begin the processes of coyly asking him to pick him up instead of taking the bus home. Robbie smiled and said "Yeah, that's when I'm bolting today, why do you ask?" Looking both directions Alex said "Well I was wondering. I mean if we are still going to 'relax' later, I just thought it made sense to pick me up and we could go to your place from there."

"Gee Alex, what if I haven't been a successful shopper today, that could be a problem huh? I'm just saying that would suck", said Robbie wanting to draw out the torment. "What?" asked Alex as he was sure that others could detect the crescendo in his voice with that simple word as panic quickly sank in and he began a brief tirade "But you promised that it would be a sure thing today. Dude this is not cool, not right now!" Once again staring at the crowd that had begun boarding the bus that had just arrived, Alex was sure he was drawing attention from someone with his erratic behavior and vocal outburst. But in reality not a soul noticed. Soon he was forced into making the decision to either board the bus or gamble on whether or not Robbie would come to some aide and pick him up. The bus closed its door and lumber away from the curb with a low rumble as if it were making the decision for him as Alex exclaimed, "Fuck the bus just left and I'm hurting. You have to help me out here. Come on man."

Robbie now laughing on the other end of the line said in jest "Man, calm down. You know I'm fucking with you, Jesus Christ get a grip." The moment of silence that had suddenly occurred reminded Alex that he had very much become a slave to this addiction of his and was both ashamed and angry. The anger was in the question of why he felt so needy to it as Robbie treated it as a love he could walk away from as more abdominal cramps passed through Alex, this time at higher intensity.

In the time since the two had been hanging out Robbie never had the levels of desperation that Alex did. "Ok buddy where are you?" asked a sympathetic Robbie with a hint of sarcasm to his voice. Looking up Alex read the street signs and said "13th and South Michigan Avenue." He wasn't sure why he looked up since this was the corner that he caught the bus from almost every day but he enjoyed the added security of knowing he gave his exact location. "Yeah I know where that's at, give me thirty minutes or so and I'll be there" said Robbie trying to get off of the line and as if Alex needed the added comfort asked "You did get it right?" "Jesus yes I got it!" snapped Robbie before abruptly hanging up on his drug buddy.

This final exchange left Alex speechless and taken back as to how he let people treat him this way. Since he had been standing most of the day the bench looked very welcoming to his tired legs and he felt he needed to make the best of the situation and the weather and simply sit and wait. Once sitting down Alex held his head in his hands and looked down at the cracked and aged sidewalk beneath his feet and was now relieved that he had some time to collect his thoughts and to let time wander. The candy wrapper that he had watched before his phone call with Robbie had become blown against the side of the base of the concrete bench by his right foot. His thoughts turned to this paper wrapper and how it had fulfilled its mission and long since given up its treasure, fulfilling its only purpose in life. Now it was discarded into the world and tossed by the wind to wander until disintegration. Before Alex could put more thought or over emphasis on this one piece of paper a gust of wind dislodged it from the side of the bench and carried it away.

"Days like these are really rare aren't they?" said a voice to his right. Without Alex even noticing an older gentleman had taken a seat on the opposite end of the bend, he had been too transfixed on the wrapper all of this time. It caught him off guard as he began to panic as to how to react to this stranger next to him, but upon closer inspection Alex realized that he was sitting next to a coworker from the museum. "Nice to meet you young man, my name is Donald and I do believe you and I work together", said the neighbor on the bench. Alex perked up a little but still remained on guard to this gentle older man. "Hi, I'm Alex" he said as he extended his hand and shook that of the older man with a warm smile as Donald said "And you work in the custodial department if I recall correctly." "Yeah that's right, I'm a mop jockey", replied Alex, "I started several weeks ago."

Donald reached into his beige overcoat and produced a candy bar from the pocket as he said. "Well I hope you like it after all it's a great place to work. I've been in security there for over twenty-four years." "Wow!" exclaimed Alex marveling at his tenure before adding "I can't imagine being at a place that long." Donald looked Alex in the eye and said, "Oh it's easy, you just get up every day and remind yourself that you love what you do. If you don't love it then change it. Really that's a reflection on life instead of work, but you can always apply it there too. Besides how could you not love where we work?" Donald playfully slapped Alex in the arm and said, "I've seen some of the most amazing things mankind and mother earth have to offer up. Plus I get to see kids and the looks on their faces as they see mummies and dinosaur fossils and who knows what else the folks at the top of the ladder are going to get in next? The kids are great, but some can be total brats." As he finished his statement on the kids the laugh and the smile told Alex that he meant no harm in what he said and only had the best intentions behind his thoughts and actions.

Clearly Donald did not fit the usual description of a security guard, his hair was a combination of whites and darker grays, or that is what remained of it. And his eyes were a warm brown that were welcoming to everyone he crossed paths with. "But the brats are a small price to pay, you take the crunchy with the smooth" added Donald as he gazed out into the passing cars and said "I'll miss them six months from now, that

I'm sure of." Alex become even more uneasy as he was unsure as to whether or not Donald would notice his behavior and alert his employer about any suspicions, but this uneasiness was briefly put on hold as Donald laughed and said "Sit still young man, life is too short to be all wound up like that."

Alex had not noticed the degree of his own rocking back and forth and how his hands were shaking as he readied himself for more waves of cramps. It was like looking at the calendar and knowing tomorrow will happen it's just a matter of time and sometimes a distraction is the best remedy so to counter this Alex asked, "What's happening in six months?" "Oh they call it mandatory retirement, but I call it bull" said Donald resting his chin in his upturned palm with his elbow on his knee. Donald shifted his attention to Alex and said, "Do you know that there are kids that toured that place so much year after year and they remember me into adulthood? All of those field trips let me meet a lot of great teachers and students over and over. I always did try to be the personable type to the groups coming in."

Sighing Donald smiled and said "I just need to remember the thirty-four years and be happy with that, but I still won't know what to do with myself when I get up in the morning." Returning the arm tap from earlier

Alex playfully smacked Donald in the arm and said, "The ring on your finger says you have a wife, travel with her or something" his breathing remained staggered as he finished his statement. Donald looked at his ring and said "Oh that might be difficult, Martha's been gone for over three years now." Alex shifted on the bench and expressed his regret over his error in judgment. "Oh, no harm young man, I always wear the ring because it reminds me of her. She was as you kids would say 'awesome'" said Donald smiling. Alex could tell that he had nothing be happy thoughts passing through his head as they both looked upon the gold band on the aged finger. "Surely you must have a special someone too?" asked Donald not wanting to dwell too long.

The question caught Alex off guard as Donald could clearly see on his face and he said, "Well I was seeing someone, but she moved on." Donald thought a little damage control was in order as he replied, "I can see it's a sore spot, I'm sorry." For the first time Alex noticed his physical actions had ceased and he felt comfortable in his skin but also realized that he had reached the eye of the storm and such comfort was only fleeting. "Oh don't be sorry, I was a jerk and she just deserves better, it's that simple. Besides I see Samantha about once or twice a month and sometimes more, we're cool trust me." As Alex finished his sentence he thought for a second about the real reason she broke it off and how it was all on him and how he had failed to live up to his end of the deal and 'clean up'. That was her ultimatum and he made his choice. It also crossed his mind how Robbie despised Samantha and assassinated her character at every chance. Donald made a comment on how it was good to maintain a friendship as he looked Alex in the eye and read further into the situation than Alex knew.

A car backfired off in the distance and shook the younger of the two men as Alex jolted on the bench and a glaze of sweat created a sheen on his forehead. "Like I said early son you have to relax. Are you ok?" asked Donald unflinching in the aftermath of the small contained explosion. Alex held his right hand over his heart and attempted to calm himself although he knew it was a losing battle. Donald then put his hand on the shoulder of the young man and again inquired "Are you sure you're ok? You look fairly flush."

Alex continued to assure Donald he was fine as he glanced repeatedly at his watch and internally begged for Robbie to arrive. He knew his erratic breathing was something alarming to the outside observer but he also knew to keep his mouth shut. Donald reached into his coat with his one free hand and produced another candy bar. "Here" he said, "You look like you need some sugar and this always does the trick with my grandson, although his mom seems to have a problem with my home cures." He accepted the Hershey's bar and put it in the inside breast pocket of his jacket and thanked Donald to which he replied "You're welcome just make sure you eat it because you're too thin."

As more time passed Alex began to wind down beside Donald as he told him stories of his years at the museum and what he had seen in his life. This however was brought to an abrupt conclusion when Alex heard two quick stabs of a car horn and noticed the four-door sedan of Robbie parked across the street. The car much like its owner had seen better days. It was a 1991 Caprice Classic that had already gone into self-disintegration through lack of up keep and being passed from one abusive owner to another. Alex stood as though on command and said "I have to go, my ride is here."

Just the sight of that car was a reminder of the angst within Alex and the cure located within its interior as he could clearly see Robbie passing stares between his watch and Alex standing beside Donald on the bench. As if Donald could sense the strain on Alex he reached out caught the edge of the green wind breaker on Alex and asked "Once again I'm going to butt in, are you okay?" This time his stare and tone were more fatherly than before, both authoritarian and caring in nature. "I'm fine, he just hates to be kept waiting, you know, the very impatient type" said Alex as he began to step away. Donald stood and watched Alex dodge cars as he crossed the street and then raised his voice to say "I'd better see you at work tomorrow the Civil War exhibit opens!"

The closer Alex got to the car the more he noticed the flaws. The dark metallic blue was sun faded and had lost its luster and in sporadic places gray primer was visible covering up poorly crafted body repairs. The wheel wells had started to rust out and it was missing most of its emblems, and although it didn't have a loud exhaust the engine struggled to maintain a steady idle as though it were choking to death. All of this became more visible to Alex the closer he got until he was within 15 feet and Robbie broke his attention by coldly saying "Hurry up and get it."

His mannerism towards Alex was over powering as he knew Robbie had what he needed and within the hour both would be stoned. Alex rounded the front of the car until he reached the passenger side door and attempted to open it. He struggled for about fifteen seconds before he saw Robbie lean across the bench seat to pull the interior latch to open the door. Alex knew he always had trouble operating this door and Robbie always had to open it for him, still he always let Alex make attempt after failed attempt.

The full body weight of Alex came down on the front seat of the car and Robbie held up a clenched fist and asked, "Buddy, what is up with you and that damn door?" Alex balled up his fist and lightly touched the knuckles against his friends as he said "Operator error, now get me out of here" as Robbie dropped the transmission into drive and the engine strained under the load of the car. Alex rubbed his forehead and fought the beginnings of a headache and looked over at his friend as he just missed clipping the bumper of the car in front of him by two inches. Robbie wore the same dingy jeans and flannel shirt he always did at the warehouse job. He also had the added luxury of not having to shave on a regular basis and sported facial hair that was long and hardly kept in shape, but not quite a full beard. He also kept his oily black hair in a ponytail that measured in at 10 inches. He too noticed that Robbie always smelled of exhaust, the aroma would follow the man no matter how much he bathed or how hard he tried to escape it. His observation of his friend was broken as Robbie said, "So how's the fucking museum gig anyway? Just swipe some of the Egyptian crap and you'll never have to work again."

"Yeah, because my ass will be in jail" replied Alex taking note of the filth in the car and the faded cloth on the head rests. This got Robbie to laugh as he said "Then you'd have to suck dick for 'h', or whatever it is they do in there to get a fix." His laughter was ceased by the ringing of his cell phone and he reached into his pocket to find it. "Bitch" was the first thing Robbie said as he looked at the small screen. This reaction could have been produced by any of two-dozen females that Robbie chose to associate with so Alex waited to let him solve the mystery. "Gina you bitch, it's like she knows when I'm holding. That bitch has radar I swear to fucking God" as he slapped Alex in the arm. This reminder and contact with his arm made Alex swiftly turn his head and locked eyes with Robbie to non-verbally express his increased desperation. The driver shifted the attention off of his sad passenger and back to the road before pointing back at Alex and saying, "Man you look like shit, but not to worry Doctor Robbie is here."

All Alex could do was think of how much relief putting that needle in his arm would bring so he thought the best course of action would be to talk about other subjects in the meantime. Unfortunately the first topic at hand was poorly chosen as Alex said, "I haven't seen Gina in a while, how is she?" Robbie shook his head and said, "A total pain in the ass, but good where it counts if you get my drift?" Again Robbie slapped Alex in the arm and added to his monologue on Gina, "At least she knows where she stands with me, a fix and fucking and that's it. Three things about her, get high, get off, and get out." Again his laughter started and Alex thought to himself how sad it was that they shared a car, a common destination, and a common desire.

Alex could tell that they were entering an area close to Robbie's apartment and recognized the older brick buildings and vacant lots. "You see that's your problem, you see girls and think 'oh, they want to be my friend' other than bitches wanting something" said Robbie navigating through the south side of Chicago his eyes shifting from the left to the right. This jaded view of the opposite sex was always a debated point between the two as Robbie mumbled under his breath "bitches." Alex showing very poor judgment blindly asked, "How come you never liked Samantha anyway?" This was a hot button with Robbie and he held nothing back in his opinion of her. "Oh fuck her, where to start with that crazy bitch?" exclaimed Robbie throwing his hands into the air as if shocked by the question but still welcoming the opportunity verbally degrade her.

He never made it a secret how he felt about the former object of Alex's desire but did not know how concentrated the return feeling was from Samantha, she just chose her words and moods with much more precision and care. She also chose to put her energy into Alex rather than attacking other. The restless passenger decided he'd switch the stereo on to hopefully take their minds off of this subject but to no avail as Robbie began talking over classic rock as dull as the blue paint on the car. Alex felt a stinging slap to his chest as Robbie got his attention. The hand that just made contact was now used to direct all attention to his eyes. Although they were still driving and in motion Robbie held his hand up and spread his fingers to form a 'v' in front of his face with the finger tips on front of each eye.

"Dude, I say this as your friend, knock off the fem attitude before you grow a pussy" said Robbie in a rather acidy tone before adding "Plus that sensitive male bullshit gets real old too." The two became quiet as Alex was once again ashamed of himself as he sat next to Robbie, the dominance was unquestionable. Somehow this embarrassment brought clarity to Alex and he made sure not to bring up any subjects that were female related. He often wondered how he fell into such social trappings and wondered why he wasn't as sharp as he once was.

He honestly missed the games he and Samantha would

play with words. Sometimes before a date or an outing they would each chose 10 words from the thesaurus or dictionary for each other and insist that they use them in everyday interaction with people they would meet. One such memory was when he was forced to use the word "pornotopia." Although it was a coined word the challenge was accepted. He had already gone through the list supplied by Samantha and wanted to complete his before she did, so he simply asked the waiter at a café "Is there a pornotopia around here?" Later this brought protest from Samantha as she stated "Anyone could simply be an idiot with these words, but the true test is to use them with thought." Of course Alex fired back by sarcastically asking, "Well what kind of word is 'pornotopia' anyway? Oh wait, it's perverted slang isn't it?"

The simple act of daydreaming about this piece of his past did Alex some good and he laughed to himself, but not quietly enough that it didn't arouse the attention of Robbie. "Hey what's so fucking funny?" he asked sternly to which Alex chuckled and said "Oh nothing, just pornotopia, it's a long story. So what did you buy us today?" Robbie looked over with a sly smile and squinted eyes and said "Well I got you the usual, but I splurged on myself and went big time high quality top shelf shit. And no you can't have any." Robbie began smacking the steering wheel with both hands while stomping with his left foot and laughing. The only response Alex could muster was "Whatever, as long as I've got mine" to which he was once again embarrassed by the lack of creativity in his retort. "Oh don't be upset if I can afford the good stuff, I work my ass off so I deserve it", said Robbie as he began search his pockets for what Alex could only assume was a cigarette as he asked Robbie "Hey, what happened to that promotion they were talking to you about?"

As if Alex had the hidden talent to bring up the worst subjects Robbie was once again dejected and said, "Christ man, what is it with you?" From there a small argument ensued about Alex and his pension for bringing up various subjects at the worst time as he tried to apologize. "Ok, get this man, it's way fucked up. They spent three weeks pumping me up for this promotion and then they hit me with the 'you have to take a piss test' line" explained Robbie as they pulled into the parking lot of his apartment building and continued with "Well fuck that! I'd get my ass fired and then I'd be pushing a broom with you or some shit like that, no thanks."

As the two made their way through the compound of pale beige colored vinyl two-story buildings Robbie showed no remorse for his callous statement towards Alex and his job, it was as if he were devoid of the emotions that others felt. Some windows were complete, some knocked out and covered with particleboard and some of the same cars were still in their usual places. In the time in which the two had become associated on the level of friendship or just to get high at Robbie's place Alex had never seen some of the cars ever leave their parking spaces, they simply went nowhere and rotted before his very eyes.

Robbie reached under his seat and said in a voice that echoed of excitement "Fuck yeah! Smokes!" He then produced a crumpled pack of cigarettes and quickly put one in his mouth only to have his feelings dashed upon discovering that his car lighter was not functioning. "Shit! Why does nothing work?" he said smacking his dashboard as the action startled Alex and he jumped in his skin. The car forcibly pulled into a vacant oil stained parking spot in front of the apartment belonging to Robbie and the two quickly unlatched their seat restraints and exited the car.

These two knew the euphoria that waited once they got inside and Alex was no longer interested in the perfect whether outside. "Hey man, you got a lighter?" asked Robbie as they both walked in a quick stride and Alex began to pat himself down, he started at his pants pockets and worked his way up to his windbreaker. He then felt a thin stiff rectangular object in his jacket pocket and said "Hey wait, I think I have one." Both men stopped as Alex unzipped his jacket and reached in only to present the candy bar given to him by Donald. Robbie began to berate Alex about stopping him over a candy bar before saying "I'll be inside" and stomped off leaving Alex alone and distracted just short of the steps leading up to the apartment.

He stood there comforted by the memory of visiting with Donald and how the man's voice and gestures made Alex seem less uptight, even at ease even as his body was beginning to scream for the drug it so badly needed. And again he was taken aback by the comfort provided by this mere artifact of that meeting. For a second he wished he had the strength to turn around and find a bus stop and just go home for the evening and even for a second he did possess that strength but only to discover that it was fleeting. As if under the spell of a darkness that controlled his every motivation he shamefully began climbing step by step towards the door and Robbie's pitiful apartment.

CHAPTER 2

Alex caught up with Robbie at the top of the stairs as he turned the key to his apartment and the maroon door easily swung open to reveal a simple one-bedroom dwelling that always had the smell of pet urine in the air. Alex grew used to this in time although he was perplexed at how this small apartment was never cleaned and never became any more disorganized and cluttered than it already was; as if Robbie had reached a comfortable level of upheaval not only in his living quarters but in his life. Neither bothered to remove their shoes as they entered and Alex sat his green jacket on the armrest and then dropped onto the dingy gray couch next to the sliding glass door. Robbie on the other hand went straight to the shelf that sat next to his television that sometimes work, other times did not. He reached up and retrieved a small red teapot and removed the lid, from there he inserted two small bags.

The clank noise told Alex that the drugs were in a safe place for the time being.

There were only two lamps in the room and only the floor model worked. Robbie reached under the shade and after several clicks it came to life and gave off a reddish glow from the shade and the single 75 watt bulb. The matching table lamp stopped working several weeks ago but from what Alex could derive it was more than likely a bad bulb but both men were never in the mindset to explore the root cause of failure once inside the tiny apartment, they always had other more pressing issues to attend to. The table lamp was perched on a cheap pressboard table of a faux oak finish with a matching coffee table and shelves. It seemed to be the only items of furniture in the place that made any sense and that were purchased at the same time; everything else was piecemealed together over time. The plastic horizontal blinds that covered the sliding glass door were torn and slightly shredded, as too were the blinds in the single window in the room. The dwelling was overall dark and that's the way Robbie preferred it, he did not want voyeuristic neighbors investigating his activities.

"Ah home sweet shit hole", said Robbie stretching skyward before as he verbally offered Alex a beer from the refrigerator. "Sure, that'd be great" he replied before he called for the dog that Robbie owned. Emerging from the kitchen with two shiny aluminum cans of beer Robbie said, "Dude, save your breath, Reno's not here anymore." "Why's that? He was cool," replied Alex looking at Robbie in a perplexed fashion as a beer was exchanged and opened. Alex always liked the company Robbie's dog Reno. He was a mutt, every ounce from tip to tail and always very full of energy, and aside from the high Alex would experience in Robbie's company seeing the dog was always something he looked forward too. The way he seemed to have boundless energy or a simple love of life that in a way inspired Alex.

"The dog was too much trouble, always fucking the place up and shit, just too much trouble", said Robbie pointing out various areas of his apartment that had been destroyed and had the evidence of claw marks to prove it. Alex quickly came to the defense of Reno by saying "That was a cool dog, and you never took him for walks, what did you expect?" The retort from his guest aggravated Robbie as she took a swig of beer and said "Fuck if you want him he's at Animal Control, not my problem anymore." Statements like this not only hit Alex hard but made him wonder why he chose this sad cruel man as company until he felt the stirring inside of him that could only be calmed with heroin, the cramps had once again returned and made him wince in pain.

The humiliation was too much for Alex as he struggled to say, "I just liked Reno" and took a drink of the cheap beer Robbie kept on hand as the aching in Alex increased as his body knew of the relief coming. Robbie held his beer in the air and said, "To Reno, trust me he won't feel a thing and neither will we so let's do this!"

This was a clear indication that it was time to get down to the act in which they had come to do. The impact of the last sentence about Reno was now lost on Alex as his attention was turned to Robbie who had stood and was now walking across the room to the shelf by the television. Once again the clanking noise was like music to his ears and his friend removed the porcelain top and retrieved the powdered treasure from within. The top was put back in place as Robbie spun around and said, "What I have here are two goodie bags, yours and mine" as he held two small zip lock bags in his hand. The scale of the bags he held gave Robbie the appearance of a giant. The bag in his left hand contained a powered with the color of brown sugar, this was what Alex was used to seeing and there were no surprises. The bag held in his right hand contained a powder that was so white it glowed in the dim light of the apartment, as if it were a beacon calling out to Alex and he being a lost ship and it was the desired salvation. There was no doubt of the quality it held over the average or even inferior product in the left hand.

"China white my friend", said Robbie smiling as if he were a proud father "And it's mine all mine" as his voice cracked with the giddiness. "Nice" replied Alex with a crooked smile as he found himself extremely jealous but managed to keep his emotions under tight wraps. The two men quickly began to assemble what they needed as Alex went to the bathroom and gathered rubbing alcohol and cotton balls from the cabinet and Robbie went to his bedroom and pulled a small wooden cigar box from his dresser before his hurried return to the living room. Alex had already removed his jacket, set his cell phone on the small table, and had begun rolling up the left sleeve of his gray button down shirt. Robbie carefully set the wooden box on the coffee table and went back into the kitchen where Alex could hear the sound of the sink running as he filled a drinking glass with water and then the metallic shuffle of silverware. Returning once again Robbie put the glass of water on the table with a shiny tablespoon. Alex spun the top off of the rubbing alcohol as the pungent smell reached his nose for the first time. He used to associate the smell with all things medical, but like a Pavlovian dog he now only became excited by the scent and what was to follow.

Robbie had just sat down Indian style across from Alex when his phone began to ring. "Fuck" was the only thing Robbie said as he fell back and added "Not now, not fucking now." Hoisting himself back up Alex pled with him not to answer it as he went on to say "Dude, whatever it is it can wait." Robbie could see the desperation in the eyes of his friend, how he not only longed for but intensely craved the powder in the bags as they sat side by side on the table, one more pure and more potent than the other. This was going to be another perverse example of the power Robbie had over Alex as he said, "I think I'll get that, don't touch my shit" with a cruel smile.

Alex hung his head and ran his fingers through his hair as Robbie began the usual phone greeting before he sounded a little more exuberant by saying "Gina! Hey baby what's going on?" there was a pause and Alex had the faint and growing feeling that this maybe a longer wait as from across the room he heard "I'm here with Alex getting ready to kick back for a while, you game?" Again more silence as the tension inside Alex began to climb and his heart rate increased. "Cool, very cool" said Robbie as Alex looked up for the first time and noticed Robbie was watching his every move and reaction to the phone call taking place and loving the torment he was causing. "You sit tight and I'll be there soon, I have some good stuff today, you'll love it" he said before hanging up without the usual ending salutations that conclude a phone conversation.

Alex let out a deep breath as Robbie said "Don't hate my friend, be glad that at least one of us is getting laid today, I just have the better party favors." He slipped his jacket back on as Alex found the remote and turned on the television hoping to take his mind off the pain continuing to growing inside of him. Robbie was pointed towards the door and quickly strode past the coffee table stopping three steps beyond and came to a complete halt. He sharply turned around and picked up the two small plastic bags and put them in his pocket and for a moment became lost in thought. He then removed the two bags and returned them to the teapot on the shelf before saying "I don't feel like leaving the house with that so I'm ditching it here. If anyone breaks in kill them", said Robbie with a laugh. Alex stretched and didn't even look at Robbie as he continued watching television and said "Sure thing" in a far off voice. Robbie felt the need to make a further impression on Alex as he said "Oh, one other thing. If you touch my shit I will kill you. Got it?"

The finger now pointing at Alex and the tone in his voice sent a clear message of how serious he was as the red hue from the lamp shade gave his face a sinister appeal. "Yeah man, don't worry and get Gina", said Alex with the finger still pointed his direction. As if Robbie had a moment of either clarity or guilt for his actions he threw his hands up and said, "I didn't mean to be a dick, but it's just that. Well you can't shoot while I'm gone. You'll screw it up or something." It normally wasn't in his mannerism to care about how he left people but he was hoping this tactic would somehow smooth things over while he was gone. The truth was that Alex struggled with the proper mixture. As long as he had been doing this he still had yet to master the proper ratio of water and powder.

The onset of cramps could now be felt in the abdomen of Alex and he put up a strong effort to mask his pain and curled up into a tight ball. "Just go, I'll be here when you get back", said Alex as he began biting the inside of his lower lip. Robbie agreed and once again mentioned he would be back soon and he might stop for some fast food and he'll bring Alex something if he did. The act of kindness a rare gesture. The focus of Alex returned to the television as off in the distance he heard the sound of car keys and the lock being thrown on the door as Robbie left Alex alone with the company of a terrible sitcom through worn out device. Once the door was safely closed Alex turned the television off and doubled over on the couch and moaned. He knew that this pain was a possibility and even anticipated it, but not to this degree as he stood and made his way to the bathroom to put water on his face.

The walk was short in distance but long in struggle, and upon entering he paid little attention to the filthy tiled floor with dog hair and a mound of dirty clothes. The facet handle was in the palm of his hand and made a screeching noise as Alex turned it to the right and cool water flowed into the sink as he cupped his hands beneath the rushing stream. A sharp pain coursed through his stomach and he doubled over in agony knowing he had gone too long without what his body had craved and Alex also knew that the worst was yet to come. As he regained his stance and steadied himself on the sink basin, he then splashed the water onto his face hoping the cool sensation would sharpen his focus. But this was to no avail as he sank to the floor with his back against the bathtub, he neglected to turn the water off and listened closely for only a second as the shifting sound of increasing and decreasing in pressure from the tap. This too was not enough to distract him as yet another wave of cramps racked his body, this time three in quick succession.

Alex drew his knees to his chest in and formed a tight ball, the muscles acted as if it were the only action they knew or were capable of as his breathing became shallow and he wished Robbie were there to make it better. Robbie always knew the proper dosage and always made sure both were taken care of and safe, or as safe as one could be in this activity. Never had these symptoms set in so quickly or with such fierceness as they were now. Alex began to notice his clothes were becoming damp from sweat so he unbuttoned the shirt he had on from work only to reveal the plain white t-shirt underneath. From there his could see the military dog tags he wore.

He never served, but they belonged to a close friend. In his weakened condition Alex started to rationalize the one thing Robbie forbid him to do, shoot up alone. Although he had witnessed Robbie prepare the drugs many times in the past he didn't pay close very attention but felt he could still obtain the desired goal by himself. From his perspective in the bathroom he could see into the living room and the shelf where the teapot sat. He could just glimpse the red spout, but that was enough to call out to him, that the contents are to be his savior and he would have to explain to Robbie at a later time the degree of desperation he felt.

Alex began to stand but was forced to sit on the edge of the dirty bathtub with a dull film of soap scum. After a brief moment to calm down he felt as though he had reached another eye of the storm and took the opportunity to stand and walk to the sink still as it churned away and he grabbed the plastic tumbler off or the counter to fill it. His journey back to the living room was even more of a struggle than the first trip. He was forced to stop once as the pain ripped through him and he doubled over once again and dropped the plastic cup to the floor as water shot in all directions. This sudden return of agony was something he didn't expect so quickly and Alex began to weep due to the pain and knew he had to continue, it was the only solution he knew would work. His head shifted back up and the teapot stood out, now almost fully in view.

By doubling his pace Alex stood before the shelf and swiped the teapot like a greedy thief in a jewelry store heist. The grab was sloppy but the objective was achieved and the small pot was in his shaking sweating hands. The middle cushion on the couch gave into his weight as he landed with force bouncing upward ever so slightly before he stabilized and his mind was all about the teapot, cigar box, glass of water, alcohol and swabs, and the shiny spoon. Opening the box to reveal most of the items one would need for an injection and he steadied himself again as he could feel the pain beginning to roll through him, as if his body would not let up until the need was met.

He quickly removed the rubber tube from the box and laid it across his lap before removing the lid of the teapot and blindly grabbing both bags of powder. The heroin that Alex was going to use was as it always was, somethings never seem to change even as his world slowly crumbled, the bigger picture is always lost in these times. The other bag however contained a little more than usual and was pure white, Alex didn't need anyone to tell him that is was very potent compared to the lesser quality he was to take. As to not fuel his temptation and do something he would regret Alex put the bag intended for Robbie back into the pot and grabbed a syringe from the box, needles always made him nervous but he always found a way around that fear in these moments.

Shooting up solo was something he had never done and also knew that he needed to be quick and careful not to make a mess and also to appease his body. The rubber tube was strapped around his left arm twice and then tied off as Alex watched his veins rise from his flesh to the surface, the evidence of previous injections now became more noticeable and he knew he needed to find a new vein of entry. Next Alex grabbed a cotton ball and the rubbing alcohol and applied it to the puffy white ball and then rubbed his arm in the general targeted area. Cleaning the syringe was the next order of business as the cotton ball still damp was now shining the chrome tip. His gaze became so concentrated on the needle that it glowed like a lone star in a black sky. Setting the needle on the coffee table Alex grabbed the cushion with both hands and knew what was coming. The pain had now morphed into something like that of a train, one that could be heard in the far off distance and could not be stopped. The whistle would blow and the tracks would only shake and twitch slightly at first until the crescendo was beyond measure and the full pressure and pain bore down. Alex moaned and screamed as the wave crashed into him and he was forced to bend over and ride out the agony.

Severe was not the proper description for what Alex was going through as all of this was unexplored sensations and trails of hell. The incentive was now greater than ever to curtail this problem of mass proportion. The needle tip was now dunked into the glass of water and he drew liquid in the cavity of the syringe and for the first time noticed his mental note taking for this procedure was lacking. Once he felt he had the proper amount Alex rested the vessel safely on the table he opened the small bag of brown heroin and emptied it onto the spoon as he steadied his trembling hands, the left hand held spoon as the other picked the syringe back up and emptied the contents into the concave portion of the utensil. The tip was used to stir the brown powder and water together so that an optimal mix combination was achieved. Time was of the essences and the needled was back on the table and the free hand quickly dove into the cigar box to find the trusty Zippo lighter always used during this procedure, which had managed to become hidden under some rolling papers.

The flame leapt forth from the chrome lighter as he wasted no time in bringing the spoon and lighter together to cook the drug into a potent medicine. Alex gently waived the small torch under the spoon and noticed how bubbles would form and the hue of the mixture turned a little darker, this was the one step he always paid attention too, as if he were a child anticipating cookies to complete their baking processes, Alex knew when it was ready. An incent burner from the corner of the table was used to steady the hot spoon as he was careful not to spill any of the precious liquid. The Zippo was dropped on the tabletop and produced a loud 'thud' before bouncing off and landing out of view on the floor below as every fiber of his being was concentrated on the syringe as he picked it up and blindly filled it with no regard to quantity.

The veins in his arm seemed to be like hungry koi in a pond knowing it was feeding time and each showing off as to why they deserved it more than the other. He spotted a fresh entry point and sunk the polished tube into his flesh, the pain was something he had grown used to and didn't bother him in the least as he took in the moment of the warm drug being forced into his body from the pressure on the syringe. Alex drew in a sharp breath as a sudden cramp assaulted his stomach and knew the agony was almost over with for the day as he began the usual 10-second count down to wait for the outright euphoria to begin. Without bothering to remove the rubber tube from his arm the needled was placed upon the table and he stretched out on the couch and took satisfaction in the feeling of the pain leaving his body. To him it was as if he had vanquished a foe.

Finding an object to blankly concentrate on was usually how Alex began most trips and from the couch he scanned the room hoping to find something of interest before the full effect hit him almost instantly. The search took his swiveling head and shifting eyes back to the kitchen as the drug began to work its magic a little more and Alex took aim at a bag of garbage sitting next to the dishwasher. It was a plain white plastic bag tied off at the top and Alex studied the various shapes and forms being made from the contents inside. Nothing of great importance stood out except for what appeared to be a bowl towards the bottom. Never had he wittiness Robbie throw away any kitchen items and the size now intrigued him. After a little more study it dawned on him that the previous user of the bowl was Reno.

Floating and free was the sensation Alex was experiencing at the moment his heart sank looking at the bag of trash ready to be taken away. The drug made him selfish at that point and he chose to close his eyes and shift his attention towards his inner thoughts as his head turned to face the ceiling. Several minutes had past and this was when he realized that the pain had not completely left; only briefly disappeared like an actor might do off stage before waiting for their moment to return to the spot light. The carefree feeling he once felt so strongly was not in the full force it used to be and he knew the dreaded tolerance to the drug had started to set in. Robbie had warned him that this could happen and the only cure would be a more potent medication. Thoughts traversed his mind about how he would pay for and obtain more heroin, he knew he did have a little money in the bank and payday was soon, but the need was greatly upon him. With his eyes open Alex searched his pockets for his phone to contact Robbie, he tried to move as little as possible for fear of disturbing the high he had.

He had the strength to activate the phone but lacked the will to dial Robbie in his time of need; it was as if Alex could predict the denial that would arise from asking Alex to find more of the drug he needed to calm his soul. Alex then dropped his phone to the floor as he then surveyed the room for any more distractions. This only revealed nothing expect the red teapot being the most obvious fixture. Temptation began to grow in Alex as he in verbatim recalled the threat made against him if he dared to disturb the China white that Robbie had purchased.

As if his mind briefly shut down for a moment to cease all rational thought his body took over and Alex sat up and grabbed the small bag from the teapot. The rubber tube was still around his arm and the veins were still prominent under his flesh. Biting his upper lip Alex then shook his head in disappointment and anger towards himself succumbing to this weakness that had been growing for months while slowly sneaking up on him. "Goddamn", mumbled Alex as he began the process once more, this time with the stronger powder. 'I just need a little' he thought to himself, 'but how much?' knowing full well that this was a much higher quality than his normal dosage, and also wanting to not leave his friend with nothing. Alex emptied a third of the bag into the spoon and added less water this time, he had a grasp of what he was doing but in reality was not up to the task. After the lighter had brought the potion to life he hurriedly drew the combination up into the body of the needle and plunged it into his arm.

The drug was expeditious in its mission as it coursed its way through the body of Alex mixing with blood and soul to deliver a feeling he had never felt before. Love and sex were but mere ghosts of emotions that could never compare to this moment as he let out a deep breath and went limp on the couch and fought to pull the rubber tube away from his arm, he was positive it was no longer needed. With his eyes nearly closed he enjoyed the light show creeping into his cracked eyelids and drew in breath after breath noticing how sweet it tasted. Never before had the air been laced with such flavor and it was beyond description. The world had also become muted and he was grateful to his ears for keeping out the sounds of disturbance, the everyday outside world. Although he was unaware of his facial expression he was sure it must have been a reflection of bliss.

This feeling persisted for a little while longer and Alex felt like a leaf in a steam being carried away. Then the drug began to turn. The waters had become turbulent and he felt nauseous as his stomach started trembling and cramping. Getting to the bathroom was the first thought that went through his head as his first attempt to stand was cut short and he fell down onto the couch as he discovered his legs were of no use. The force of the impact on the couch pushed back on his body and he rolled over onto the floor while striking the coffee table and removing half the items from the surface to the floor, the teapot somehow managed to hold its ground. Like a fish kicking for life Alex tried to make heads or tails of the strange world in which his limbs refused to work in. What was horizontal was now vertical and he struggled to pull himself on his elbows towards the bathroom. He marveled at how far away the room seemed and how rough the carpet felt even in his drugged state.

Since Alex had not eaten lunch that day his stomach had nothing to expel, still it didn't stop it from trying. The dry heaves had now started as he rolled onto his side and drool poured from his open mouth. Wave after wave hit him and he noticed his heart flutter from its normal pattern, one minute it would race to where it would burst from his chest, the next slow to a crawl and he would be calm. At the end of the hall after the entire struggle he was now presented with two choices, the bathroom on the right and the bedroom of Robbie on the left. On his back Alex was covered in sweat and turned his head from one room to the other trying to decide. Tunnel vision sat in as he now could see the cordless phone on the side table by the bed and knew the choice had been made.

It took every ounce of strength Alex had to rollover onto his side and then stomach and continue his trek towards the phone as he was now fully aware of his desperate state with his legs now growing numb. While on the floor he was now presented with a new obstacle as he felt his vision failing and he could not completely feel with his fingertips, but some sensations were still there. He would have moments of a pitch-black existence knowing his eyes were open to the world. Relying on memory and then moments of returned vision he was now lengthwise on the dirty floor with his position being next to the bed. Above his head was the nightstand with the phone he now needed more than anything in his life, he needed to call for help. Alex closed his eyes in an attempted to clarify his vision and was only more dishearten upon opening to see the world in a fuzzy state with a florescent quality.

His left arm went under the bed as his right arm was halfway extended to reach for the phone, but every time would return to him failing in its mission. The left had meanwhile found a rubber ball that had been lost under the bed and there were the unmistakable teeth marks and indentions that told Alex whom this ball belonged to. Every time he tried to reach the phone he would fail from lack of strength and focus, he also noticed he was now going to sleep and having brief dreams about people he had never before met. Each dream would be out of focus and he could not make out any faces of these strangers that stood nearby but did not speak, he also took note of how these beings glowed in a soft haze and how they were the only light source and that there was no discernible landscape as it was all dark.

After every experience he would suddenly wake up and concentrate on the phone until after the forth such occurrence, and then he contemplated giving into the need to sleep, it felt so welcoming that he surely felt he would be foolish not to engage in this tempting slumber. As if being held up be a million small hands Alex felt as though he were being passed from person to person and traveling in a smooth pace, but understanding he was physically still. Again the dreams started as a semi awake Alex looked up at a blurry person now staring back down. In his left hand he clutched the ball once used by Reno as he squeezed it with his fading strength and was hit with several rounds of bright brilliant light and then noticed the room turning from dark gray and then to black. Alex was then still as his watch struck 5:55 pm.

CHAPTER 3

Traffic congestion had spilled over from the nearby interstate system and into the side streets as Robbie forcefully drove his ailing car to Gina's residence with the warning lights flickering and glowing in a way that would surely make a jukebox jealous. This traffic should have been no surprise to Robbie and had known from years of experience that this was a way of life during this time of day and in this section of the city. Still the very predictable and yet somehow forgettable backup in traffic now bothered him as he struck the steering wheel out of frustration as he was either too proud or too ignorant to admit his lack in judgment, so instead he chose to mumble obscenities at passersby and blame them for his predicament.

In the time that Robbie had known Gina he had made numerous trips to her place and always for purposes that served his own needs more than that of Gina's. Normally he could time the round trip from one apartment to the other in matter of minutes, however the slow moving vehicles and spats of grid lock now made that an impossibility. He instead chose to gauge his travel distance in certain billboards he passed on his route. Robbie always found it darkly humorous that every advertisement catered to either smoking or alcoholic products but never understood the bigger picture nor the irony in the sun faded salvation. As he passed the ripped and faded billboard making a feeble attempt to sell a brand of cigarettes that he would never purchase Robbie knew he was almost to his intended destination, this was the never changing sign attached to the side of the building where Gina resided.

Pulling the car close to the curb he put the transmission into 'park' and was dialing Gina's phone number to informer her of his arrival and to hasten her to his car. "Hey Robbie" she said answering the phone in a positive tone she always tried to provide "Where are you?" Shaking his head Robbie said, "Traffic fucking sucked, but I'm waiting outside so get out here." From the background noise on the phone Robbie could predict what Gina was about to say as if it were written in a script and rehearsed for this very moment. "I'm still getting ready so just come in", she said. This was what he expected and this had played itself out many times but it still upset him and he was never shy about expressing himself. "Fuck! Gina you fucking do this every time, I'm mean what the fuck is wrong with you?" he said into a phone that had now gone silent. Gina decided this time her actions were worth defending as she said in the politest manner she could muster "Hey, I didn't know you were going to be so late so I folded some laundry and lost track of time, it's not worth getting this upset about" as she now listen to only the sounds of the street being broadcast on the phone before saying "Hey baby, just come up." It was her best effort to diffuse the situation.

Without even saying goodbye he rudely hung up the phone and yanked the keys from the ignition and listened as the engine that moments before had struggled to run in traffic now knocked and jerked beneath the hood, as if it were clinging to life and afraid it may not be able to start again. As if that weren't enough he slammed the driver's door shut with more force than usual to announce to the whole world his spurt of rage to the situation this was then followed by an angry march to the lobby of the old building. Once inside the two telltale signs that always told him he was in the right place sank in. First was the cracked aqua blue terrazzo floor that always welcomed him and every other guest and occupant for the last eighty years. He often thought about how long it took the cracks to form and what it must have looked like when new.

But this day was different as he was too focused on getting Gina out of the apartment and back to his to place. The second sign was the smell of mildew. Always less noticeable in the lobby but sometimes over powering in the elevator no matter what time of year it happened to be. Robbie approached the brass call box and began checking for Gina's name. She always had the same place but her roommates would change from time to time, still Robbie had never taken the time to memorize the code to punch in, instead he always buzzed Gina. His finger traced its way up and down the various buttons until he stopped on the one labeled 'Reynolds/Hudson' and he then pressed down and held it for what was more than enough time to inform Gina he was in lobby. She didn't even reply as he simply heard the electronic lock on the door release.

Once through the doors he stood face to face with the lone elevator in the building. It seemed out of place being a newer piece added to the building in the last ten years. The two stainless steel doors gleamed brightly and were flanked by walls painted a pale yellow that at one time must have been beige or perhaps a brighter version of their present color. And If he looked close enough he could see how paint was applied over years of cracks in the plaster and how it gave the buildings aging lines like an elderly face or hand. He didn't have long to ponder the obvious as the bell rang and the two doors opened before he even pressed the button to summons the lift.

Another faceless stranger emerged and he quickly exchanged places with them and pressed '5'. The two doors closed and immediately Robbie was once again confronted with the strong smell of urine and mildew that was undoubtedly coming from the maroon carpet under his feet. Always between the second and third floor the lift would lurch and strain making a noise that signaled the worst but never delivered, and in time he began to take this as just another false threat in his life. Looking forward he noticed the activity in graffiti that had increased since the last time he had been here. And as hard as the building management would try to scuff and grind away the obscenities and gang symbols they would always reappear with gusto. This moment gave way to thoughts of how even though these doors are meant to be tough and maintenance free they are not immune from a determined being on a harmful mission.

In anticipation of his arrival Gina opened and cracked the door slightly so she would avoid a greeting all together and hoped he would be a bit calmer once in her place. The strong smell of sandalwood now emerged and quickly did away with any memories of the urine aroma he was just dealing with. Robbie didn't need to announce his entrance; the door did that for him with a high-pitched but short-lived squeal followed by him closing it in a more mannered way than that of his car. Once again Gina attempted to put a silver lining on this and said "Hey Robbie, be right out" although he couldn't see the dread in her eyes as she slipped a navy blue sweatshirt over her head and took a moment to reflect in the mirror as she sat at her desk which doubled as an unorganized make-up station.

The shades were pulled in the room and the side lamp made Gina's face appear like a ghost in the mirror as her skin had a major contrast against the dark sweatshirt she had just put on. She then noticed the bags under her eyes and how the older she grew the larger they became and was convinced soon she would reach a point when no amount of make-up would hide the truths of her living and the results of her pursuits. She also thought for a second about how she was looking as old as her mother and how no young woman of her age should be confronted with what Gina was now reflecting. Not wanting to keep her guest waiting any longer she quickly stood and lightly stepped into the living room with her bare feet against the hardwood floor. Knowing her place as well as she did Gina made every effort to step on certain areas of the floor that she considered to be 'dead spots' and didn't produce the sounds of a typical aging wooden floor.

Once Robbie laid eyes on Gina he decided to mount a brief attack on her lack of planning and preparedness as he threw his arms up in confusion and said, "So what gives?" The inflection in his voice was only amplified when he noticed her hair wasn't done nor was she wearing any makeup. She made the choice not to let the evening head in a negative direction and wrapped her arms around this man who never took pride in his appearance but often pointed out her short comings as Gina began hugging him hoping this would help the situation. She only felt the one arm around the small of her back and knew this was the best she could hope for. Although she had led a fairly promiscuous existence she secretly longed for affection and worked tirelessly to obtain it from Robbie, but to no avail. His motivations were much more self-centered and this was always a sobering thought as it always sank in several hours later every time the two would meet and she knew she only had herself to blame.

"So how was your day?" asked Gina as she lightly kissed him on the cheek in yet another attempt to win him over. "Oh the usual shit, you know. Put this here, take this there, nag nag nag and bitch, bitch, and more bitch," said a sullen Robbie as he scanned the place and refused to look into Gina's eyes. She took the hint and broke any physical contact and then asked him if he'd like something to drink. "No, I just want to get out of here and be at home, I have some awesome shit to try" Gina bent over to pick up a stray t-shirt that had escaped the laundry pile and said "I don't know, I got real sick last time, it scared me." With growing tension in his voice he sharply responded "Listen, I told you the first time always makes you sick. Once you get over that the rest are great."

Her experience with lighter drugs was wide and she honestly loved the way a high quality joint or an evening drinking would make her feel. The two methods of release had their own personalities and characteristics, and to her she likened them to the feeling of intercourse or simply being free. However, her one and only experience with heroin was a harsh and scary initiation into a darker world of drug use. Robbie was the one who did the mixture and injection and from the very beginning of the trip she hated the feeling. She spent the next several hours convulsing and throwing up while Robbie only sat quietly and ignored her muted cries from help.

Gina must have been in a daze for longer than she

realized as Robbie snapped his fingers and said "Hey, fucking snap out of it and get your ass ready" as the command jolted Gina back to reality and she jumped like a startled cat, her reaction only amused Robbie. She then hurried off to her bedroom to finish putting on her face and doing something with her hair as she noticed she had twisted the t-shirt into a tight coil with her hands. Sitting in the small seat at her desk she nervously fumbled through several selections of eyeliner and lipstick before stopping herself to take a moment to try and understand why he made her so nervous. Nobody in her life had this sort of effect on her, not even the landlord she had to face from time to time when she needed to explain why rent might be late. Deep down Gina thought that this man she had come to know as Robbie was a good soul, and perhaps worth the fight if she could change him for the better. Gina had a tendency to look at troubled men with a 'lost puppy' point of view and always felt that with the right touch they would change, however she had yet to prove this theory a success. But when it came down to it the two strongest bonds between the two were related to sex and drugs, however Robbie was the one that saw this and was pleased with the arrangement.

She switched on the small clock radio on her desk and began to listen to the latest pop fare as it spoke with a raspy tone through the small speaker that had long since outlived its own peak of performance and now sounded dreadful. Still this little disposable pop tune by the next forgettable singer did managed to help elevate the mood and put her in a better frame of mind as the person she was used to seeing was buried layer by layer. Being aware she was taking too long Gina attempted to work at an increased speed while still taking the time to give herself the best look possible, and in short order she saw the face of a younger happier self, one she didn't get to gaze upon often. Gina then stood rapidly and gave herself two steady mists of perfume and switched the small radio off with her only goal being to get Robbie out of the apartment and back home. As the radio died and the sound tapered off it was replaced by the sound of conversation and laughter coming from the living room, she could clearly detect the voice of Robbie and her roommate.

At a quick pace Gina made her way into the living room and found Robbie engaging in small flirtatious conversation with her roommate. He didn't detect her presence as she walked in from behind with him seated on the broken couch that made no hesitation in torturing those that dared to rest on its cushions. She watched from behind as he did his best to turn on the charm to her roommate as she cleared her throat out of jealousy and anger towards his behavior. Robbie sprang to his feet and began to wonder just how much of the exchange between himself and her roommate that Gina had heard as Robbie was somehow able to turn the situation around against Gina. "Well Gina, please introduce me to this pretty young lady in your apartment" he said as the command was delivered she spoke up to his request "Um, yeah right, Robbie, this is Victoria, Victoria this is my friend Robbie." Robbie turned to Gina and flashed a smile smacking of perversion and illicit thoughts then turned his attention back to her roommate.

Victoria was growing more nervous by the second as she stood before Robbie, her short blonde hair in a traditional 'bob' cut, her oversized dark purple winter jacket that seemed to envelope her petite frame. Robbie noticed how tan her skin was and made a joke about her wearing such a large coat on a nice spring day such as the one the entire city was enjoying. Armed with this new information of knowing her name Robbie once again turned his attention towards Victoria and extended his right hand to shake and she too extended hers although with more apprehension. The two hands met and the first thought that passed through Robbie's head was how soft and delicate she was. She seemed pure, like a fresh canvas awaiting manipulation by the artist or in this case exploitation. He began shaking her hand in a very traditional manner in the way one might great another or close a business deal. "Well it is such a pleasure to meet you Vicky", said Robbie as he began to bring her hand to his mouth to kiss. The shortening of her name and the forced physical contact were too much for her to stand as she quickly pulled her hand back and said "First off, it's Victoria, secondly that's out of line and you should know better."

In the moments following this action nobody spoke and with each passing second all felt the tension amply. Finally Robbie again flashed his smile and turned to Gina and said, "I like her, but this cat has claws." He was the type that always tried to have a snappy comeback prepared to fly at a moment's notice and with the intention of scoring points from being clever, but he lacked the ability to see and hear his one-liners as others did. Gina quickly retrieved her purse from the side table and did her best to separate Robbie and Victoria by saying "Hey, we really need to get going." "Hey baby, what's the rush Victoria just got here, I think we all should hang out" said Robbie as his eyes shifted back towards Victoria and he gazed upon her as would an animal stalking its prey. He began sizing her up and noticed how she fidgeted with the zipper on her coat but also how she was giving him a deathly stare meant to convey how serious she was about her quickly found dislike for Robbie.

"Gina, can I talk to you real quick? In your room." asked Victoria looking for an exit, and an escape from Robbie's lustful and blatant stare. Victoria took several rapid steps around Robbie as his head swiveled to keep her in view and upon reaching Gina grabbed her arm and pulled her into the small hallway and then into the privacy of Gina's bedroom. As the door closed Gina exclaimed "I'm sorry for that, he's not always like that, trust me. Robbie's a nice guy." The look of shock must have shown on the face of the young girl as she said in response "That's Robbie? That dick out there is Robbie? The one you've told me is so fucking cool, you have to be kidding" as she was now pointing towards the door in confusion and outrage. Gina decided to mount a defense of a man she knew didn't deserve such action and said, "He's had a hard day and I wasn't ready when he got here, just don't be pissed okay?" "He's totally creepy, I don't like him one bit", said Victoria removing her oversized coat and tossing it on the bed revealing a plain black cardigan and a blue t-shirt. "Really Victoria, I think you are over reacting on this one" said Gina turning her head slightly and smiling, but Victoria would have none of this as she said "Trust me I know what an asshole looks like, that's why I left Tampa. By the way, I have my half of the rent, I'll pay you when I see you tonight." Wanting to further her point Victoria then added, "That is if I do see you, who can tell what he has in mind?"

"Sweetie, trust me I've got a few years on you and I can read people, I'll be fine" said Gina unloading yet another line she knew to be either a half truth or a full blown lie. Her track record was something Victoria knew of and also knew the two had a somewhat parallel history with bad men, however Victoria was not repeating her mistakes as she said, "I really think you should stay in tonight. We can get some Chinese takeout and rent a movie or just watch TV. You know, just have a quiet evening." She made her plea as she clasped her hands together as if she were begging. As tempting as the offer was Gina had already made up her mind, getting high took precedence over any other request or responsibilities on this day. "Hey it'll be ok, I'll be back probably around midnight and then we can do something. Do you have tomorrow off?" she asked Victoria.

Again Victoria began another small protest but could tell it was falling on deaf ears as Gina said, "Oh come on, you're only twenty-one and living in Chicago. What else could someone like you want?" This was when Victoria began weighing her options as what to say and not to say, true she was young and living in a city of many offerings that many people of any age and background would love to live in, but her reason for moving to Chicago and more importantly in with Gina was motivated by a desire to slow down and maintain a more stable life. Gina then noticed the lack of any communication and took that as a sign that this discussion had concluded and walked past Victoria towards the door.

She reached out her arm one last time and brought Gina to a full halt and said, "If I wanted to hang out with that type I'd still be living in Tampa." Gina wrenched her arm away in a manner befitting a child and stated rudely, "You are not my mom, so back off. When I say I'll be ok, then I'll be ok. Got it?" This created even more tension between the two as both knew the importance of the other and never wanted to risk it over a squabble involving a guy, but in her heart Victoria felt something she couldn't ignore and made one final request by saying "Listen, I just don't feel right about this guy. He scares me" as her voice trailed off. Gina didn't justify her last request with a statement instead she quietly turned and exited the room leaving Victoria, the fluffy coat, and the smell of sandalwood behind.

Expressions of discomfort were something that Robbie rarely if ever acknowledged in Gina or anybody, but part of her really wanted him to ask if she were okay as she entered the living room. Instead she found him sitting once again on the couch with the television on and his feet kicked up on the coffee table, as if he were settled in for a stay. With her purse now in hand she said in a blunt tone, "Come on, let's go." Without evening taking his attention away from the television Robbie said "Hey babe, ask Victoria if she wants to come too, could be fun." The smile once again returned and for the first time she felt deeply disturbed by how it was brandished and by its undertow. The exact same smile that she fell for like a trap now made her question his intentions and even her own motivations. A bit more forceful now Gina said, "I really want to go, Victoria isn't feeling well" as she turned off the television and stood by the door. Slowly getting up Robbie said "Ok, I know what you want" and laughed still not bothering to see how upset Gina had become, but she decided to play along with his motivation to get him to leave with her. "Yeah, that's right" she said cocking her head and smiling in an attempt lure him closer to the door. "Come on Gina, just ask her if she wants to come, I can make her feel better," he said with a wink. With acting that should have deserved an Oscar, Gina kept up the charade and said "Let's get out of here so I can make you feel better."

Taking this as a strong indication of what was to come Robbie jumped at the door as Gina opened it and they soon found themselves in the hallway on a path towards Robbie's car. The elevator provided Robbie with a better environment to express himself as he said, "Damn girl, your roomy is hot! We should party with her sometime, so what's her story?" as he added a demented little laugh at the end. "That's not going to happen", said Gina crossing her arms in a defensive style "She's my second cousin and she just moved here." "Shit you can't hate me for trying, it must be in your family or something like that, I mean wow!" he said making her more uncomfortable. She wasn't all that surprised by his tone or intentions towards either woman and felt as though she should try and put a positive spin on things by saying "Yeah, she had a rough time so now she's rooming with me and starting a new life here, I'm kind of responsible for her."

When he heard that Robbie doubled over in laughter and when he came up small areas of spittle were present on the corners of his lips as he said in astonishment "Yeah funny, you 'responsible' for someone. Good one Gina" as more laughter followed. The elevator had reached the bottom floor and both were then confronted with people wishing to board. As they passed through the small group of people Robbie noticed the hurt and confused look on her face and decided he didn't need to upset her so badly. "Hey cheer up, I've got something new you'll like and later we can further unwind after I kick Alex out" said Robbie as the two exited the building and Gina felt the warmer fresh air and absorbed this as a little good news.

She smiled and said, "Cool, Alex is there? I haven't seen in a so long, or at least it feels that way." Gina had met Alex a few times and always liked how easy he was to get along with and felt that they must be on the same frequency. As if he could detect any sign of happiness Robbie said, "He won't' be there long trust me The fucker missed his bus so I had to pick his ass up today, looks like I'm good at that with people." The sarcasm was undeniable and was one of many emotions that began to sink in as Gina took a seat in Robbie's car. Just once she wished a man would ask her about her day, or hold a door open, or even show her some true affection. Instead she was stuck with this man next to her in a car and the hatred she had for herself for giving in and going with him.

CHAPTER 4

Bewilderment was the first real sensation to venture through the mind of Alex as he sat with his eyes firmly closed and knowing he had his head down on his arms as he wiggled his toes to search for a normal feeling in his extremities. The images that were presented to him along with the bursts of light were not something he had ever seen before in his life during a high or not, it was simply beyond anything he could dream up on his own. He attempted to crack his knuckles but was confused by the lack of the expected 'pop' that was to accompany such an act. Next he groaned as he began to stretch his legs and was now aware of the fact that he must be sitting at a table, perhaps the kitchen table of Robbie's apartment.

The yearning to stretch now over took his body as he

pointed his legs straight at a forty-five degree angle and touched his toes to the vinyl flooring while he arched his back against the chair. A yawn escaped his mouth and he thought to himself how rested and relaxed he now seemed; it was as if he had been in a deep sleep for days or even weeks. With his eyes still closed he noticed for the first time that his feet were bare against the floor and the shirt he had on was much softer than usual.

The curiosity now got the better of him as he slowly opened his eyes while still looking upward at the ceiling. In the process of running his fingers through his hair Alex was overwhelmed by the amount of light flooding his eyes. The light seemed alien in nature as his vision adjusted to the florescent white glow with the occasional full spectrum of color that would pass by like light through a prism. 'I must still be stoned' thought Alex while repositioning himself in the seat and taking notice of the white shirt he was now wearing along with plain black pants. "Damn that was good shit" he said quietly to himself as he now realized he would need to figure out a way to explain why he used a portion Robbie's stash and how Alex would pay for it.

The world around him was all but a blur but he was now sure of his location, it was the kitchen in the residence of his friend. As his head swiveled and scanned the room his attention was frozen by a figure standing in front of the sink with their back turned to Alex. He rubbed his eyes trying to bring this person into focus as they continued to stare out the window not moving as he silently wondered who it could be. The longer he looked the more details he could make out; he knew it was a female about five feet three inches tall. She had sandy blonde hair that was very short in the back and tapered in above her neck. For the life of him Alex could not place her anywhere or in any social circles that he or Robbie interacted in. After exhausting all options and going over his memory several times Alex was forced to speak even in his semi lucid and very relaxed state.

"Hey, do I know you?" asked a cautious but still somewhat outgoing Alex rubbing his face as he still was unable to gain total focus. "No. Not really" replied the stranger with a slight laugh before adding, "You know it's been so long since I have just been able to stare out of a window like this. This is just so nice to do." He was awestruck by two things; the first was how friendly her voice was. The warm tone was there without a single threat that could be detected and it seemed to put him as ease. Secondly he was puzzled as to how anyone could find anything of interest looking out of the kitchen window in this part of town. Alex then came to the conclusion that she was observing some children in the playground nearby as she said, "Kids are really great, but some can be total brats, but these kids are cool, trust me on that one. I love how they can totally appreciate the wind and sun and clouds. They aren't yet caught up in that competition that seems to ruin people. You know greed's really the core of it? But there's a time when you're a kid that it doesn't matter and you're really free. It seems like most adults lose that, but some are lucky enough to hang on to the perspective of children. It helps you get through life." To Alex she was speaking beyond what he could absorb but he did his best to keep up.

The light was still as intense as it had been but the world seemed to be a little sharper with every passing second as the woman now turned to face Alex as he sat in his chair and he took note that she wore no shoes and what appeared to be white cotton pants and a tan sweatshirt. For the first time he was able to make eye contact and was impressed at how lovely and striking her eyes were. He had never seen eyes so blue in all of his life; there was clarity and a depth there that made him feel welcome and calm. She made the four-foot walk and joined Alex at the table as she introduced herself.

Extending her right hand towards Alex she said with a smile "Hello, my name is Joanne and it's nice to meet you Alex." Her grip was not overwhelming but still firm and her hand was soft with perfect unpolished nails. The room continued to glow and pulse as Joanne pulled back the chair to the right of Alex and sat down. In his state he felt he should start with some simple questions and first up was "Are you a friend of Robbie's? Like, he should be back soon." Perhaps if Joanne and Robbie were associated he would feel better about having to explain why he was still high in her company as the question of what happen to his clothes now became very important to him.

"No, I'm not a friend of Robbie's, that I can assure you of, although I have to say the boy needs severe help" said Joanne looking around the dingy apartment. Alex was never good about reading people and mistakenly thought she was referring to the poorly kept surroundings as he replied "Yeah, look at this dump; trust me I live a little better than this." Joanne pursed her lips and turned her head and eyes to Alex and said, "It's not his apartment I'm speaking of but they say a cluttered desk is a cluttered mind. That expression is sometimes true and sometimes not, I mean I've had some cluttered workspaces but have always kept a certain level of clarity to my being, but in this case I'd have to say it's all true" before adding a giggle and lightly tapping Alex on the forearm. A brief seriousness set in as she then said "And trust me, you don't live much better than this." This slightly insulted Alex but he was always one not to turn on the offensive with anybody.

Rubbing his eyes and passing his fingers through his hair again Alex was blunt "Listen, Joanne right?" as she looked him in the eyes and nodded at the correctness of her name as he continued "I'm going to be honest here, I am kind of coming down from quite a high and I'm a little freaked out and more than likely still stoned. I don't know you and you somehow know my damn name." She smiled and said nothing as he continued, "You just show up and you aren't friends with Robbie and you're just here." She continued to say nothing but the smile disappeared and was replaced by a look of seriousness as Alex pointed to his shirt and said "And then these fucking clothes, which I don't remember so you'll have to excuse me if I'm a little alarmed right now."

Finally Joanne spoke up and said "Well Alex I know you were in drug induced state and for your information you are no longer stoned" as more silence prevailed, the look on her face told Alex that she was choosing her words more carefully, at least with more precision than he was used to in his daily interactions with most people. It was the look that was familiar to Alex or anyone that was about to receive information that could be deemed life changing. "Joanne, you seem nice, but I'm a little on edge here, you have to agree with that", said Alex tensing up. Joanne reached out and put both hands on the arm of Alex and said "Alex, I need to explain some things to you" the look in her eyes told him some explanations or declarations were coming and he remained calm as she again spoke and said "Right now I need for you to be calm and to just know that everything is okay. Something has happened and that's why I'm here."

The conversation that had begun with Alex and Joanne was cut short by the sound of keys turning a lock followed by Robbie saying "Buddy! Party time! I brought Gina." Robbie entered the apartment followed in close order by Gina, her brown hair to her shoulders, sickly pail skin, and faded jeans with a black jacket. Joanne could feel the muscle in his arm as he tried to rise and panic swamped Alex. "Oh fuck! I need to get in there, I used his stuff and I need to explain it, he'll kill me!" From the living room Robbie look down at the disarray on the coffee table and was suddenly blind with rage. The open teapot, the open cigar box, and the needle on the table were something he was willing to look past, but when he discovered the half empty bag of heroin that was meant for him it was act of treason to their friendship. "Alex you faggot! You fucking asshole!" screamed Robbie as his voice seemed to shake the walls while Alex shot to his feet. Gina stood still knowing something awful was about to happen so she instinctively excused herself to the bathroom.

"Alex! Get the fuck in here!" was the next thing being shouted from the other room and Alex stood frozen in his tracks. Joanne stood behind him and said, "He can't hurt you anymore." This was no comfort to Alex and he said in reply "He's going to kill me, I have to explain this and give him money, just something" as he heard a breaking sound and saw shards of glass fly past the door opening as Robbie was now throwing various objects in anger. As Alex began walking in the direction of the tempest Joanne once again said, "You can't go in there, we really need to talk and away from here", but there was no stopping Alex as he ventured through the door to come face to face with a man clearly out of control.

He was cautious to step over the debris field of broken glass that lay in front of him and around his bare feet. The living room that was being systematically dismantled by Robbie as Alex said, "Man I'm so sorry, I was hurting really bad. I can pay for it; I have money at my place honest!" Robbie had revenge in his eyes and Alex was frightened to know that a severe payback awaited him. He knew he was foolish in his actions, but was also man enough to try and explain them as well as offer up a plan to make it right, but fear shot through him as he had never seen a person in such a fit of rage before.

Robbie stormed passed Alex and entered the kitchen. He was puzzled as to why he wasn't detected but now concerned as for the safety of Joanne. Gina re-entered the living room hoping to make some sense of this madness and said "Baby calm down you're scaring me, it'll be okay." This had little effect as he tossed two of the chairs over and tore the pantry door open looked for Alex. This only led to more frustration and he screamed "Alex, you fucker!" and then leaned against the sink with his arms folded in an attempt to calm his nerves, as if he now realized his own heightened state of his anger. In the kitchen Alex looked at the mess and was glad to see Joanne safe as he put both hands forward and said to Robbie "Dude, calm down." For the first time he questioned why Robbie had not attacked or even noticed him. He had read stories of people being so affected by rage that they simply do not see the object of their anger and perhaps this was one of those moments. Then it occurred to Alex that he had passed through the area of broken glass without so much as a scratch to his feet.

With his hands still up in a defensive motion he cautiously looked at Joanne as she said, "Like I said we need to talk and we need to go" as Gina slowly popped her head into the kitchen to make sure Robbie was okay. "Honey you just stay here and let me check the bedroom" again no attention was paid to Alex as he muttered "Gina?" before she quickly left and Robbie punched the counter top making the dishes by the sink dance and rattle. Joanne could feel the ability to control this situation slipping away as she forcefully said in a motherly tone "Alex look at me! We need to step outside right now! As in this instant!" The look being communicated to Alex was sincere and stern and also cut short by a piercing scream form Gina. "Robbie! Robbie! Get in here now!" she said as the attention of Alex and Robbie snapped in the direction of the panic while Joanne continued to stare at Alex. Alex felt pushed by a rush of air and realized that Robbie had not only ran by him, but through part of him, it was strong enough to make him lose his balance for a brief second before regaining it and running behind Robbie as Joanne said, "Alex!" but it all fell on deaf ears.

The brief chase led through the living room and down the short hall where he had struggle to craw earlier in the day. "Oh fuck!" said Robbie as he entered his bedroom. He glanced down on Gina crying and slapping the face of the man who was lying flat on the ground. Alex was right behind Robbie and watched the events unfolding in front of him, the first thing he noticed was his shoes on this person, and then the pants that were also his. Robbie pulled a sobbing and frantic Gina to her feet and for the first time the Alex stared down and saw his own face. His skin was as white as a sheet and his eyes were still, black, and open to the ceiling. Alex tried to back away but forcefully hit the wall and asked, "What the fuck is going on here?" Joanne pulled on the sleeve of Alex and calmly said, "You were not meant to see this, come on let's go outside."

Robbie manhandled Gina as she picked up the phone to call for help, but he slapped it away from her grasp and it tumbled through the air landed out of sight. "Don't be stupid and call the cops yet! We have work to do first", said Robbie now holding Gina by the shoulders trying to calm her. "First" he said, "You need to flush the needle and those bags, even break the teapot up and flush that, okay? Look at me, got it?" She cried and nodded as he let her go and she rushed by Alex and Joanne. The feeling from before retuned to Alex and he was nearly knocked down as Gina rushed by and partially through him as Joanne was not fazed in the least by Gina passing through her. Alex held onto the trim of the door jam and was anchored in place as he said, "I don't understand any of this! What's going on?" Once again Joanne tried to coax the stressed and startled Alex from the room but he refused to budge and began to cry, or felt he may but could not get past the lump in the throat sensation. "Alex, you're not in your body anymore" Joanne said in a placid tone to Alex before adding, "You have overdosed and your body simply couldn't handle it and for all practical terms your body is dead."

Robbie straddled the chest of the lifeless Alex and lightly shook him while saying "Alex buddy, come on talk to me. Don't do this, don't be a dumb ass here." The first flush of the toilet was heard and Gina shouted "It's almost gone, call for help." Robbie took another moment to go over in his head if he had anything else in his apartment that might land on the wrong side of a jail cell. Knowing he always stored his drugs in the teapot he felt it was safe to locate the phone as he spied it on the floor in the corner. Alex watched Robbie very calmly and slowly walked towards the phone and wondered why there wasn't any more haste to his movements as he picked up the phone and placed a call to emergency services.

The three individual beeps of the phone that was being dialed seemed to take forever to begin and end as Alex put his entire focus on the phone in the hand of Robbie. Once the pace had started to bring help it would then slow down almost to a crawl. There was no reasoning for this and it went against all that he had ever known. "Who are you?" asked Alex still confused and now even more scared than a moment before. "My name is

Joanne and I've come for you, I'm not here to harm you and I only have your best interests at heart" as she placed her hand on his shoulder to once again try and extricate him from the room.

Robbie was now connected and said "Yeah, please send and ambulance now! I have a friend that has dropped dead or something!" He then gave the address to send assistance as the operator on the other end began asking the usual questions in an ill attempt to save the life of his friend on the floor. Alex knew the 911 operator would be giving Robbie advice on how to help the situation, but chose to hover over his body doing nothing. As if he felt time was slipping away from Robbie and his opportunity to clean up his apartment was diminishing he hung up then said "Gina they're on the way, make sure it's all gone!" After barking the command to Gina he leaned down over the body Robbie began going through the pockets of the still Alex and retrieved approximately $15 before looking back down and sorrowfully asking "Why man?" and left to assist Gina with any clean up in the other room. Alex watched Robbie pass through Joanne and had trouble believing what he was seeing. He now slid down the piece of door trim and rested silently on the floor staring at his body now knowing the risk was great in his actions and the price was much larger then he imagined.

She bent down in front of Alex who was now curled up in a tight ball and she said "You were not supposed to see this, some people just can't handle it" as her arms wrapped around him. "Like I said we need to talk, but here is not good" Joanne said to a shaking Alex, his body was exhibiting the emotions of someone that should be crying, but he could not produce tears as he reluctantly agreed by quietly saying "Okay." Once standing Alex put his hand on his chest to feel for the dog tags he cherished but was alarmed by the absents. "My tags, I need my tags" he said as Joanne assure him that he couldn't retrieve them and continued her push to get him outside. As they passed through the living room he noticed how slow and tense the situation had become, the energy was high but the moments and actions seemed sluggish and confusing to Alex. Joanne held the hand of the beleaguered man as they walked towards the front door and she quickly opened it and led him through to the world outside.

Before he knew it Joanne had quickly and effortlessly guided them both to the bottom of the stairs and to a nearby picnic table that Robbie and Alex used to walk by on their way into his place. The air was still and there was no wind like before, the traffic on the street had not only stopped producing noise, it had ceased to exist and not a car could be seen. It was as if all of the activity of the world had vanished leaving just the two at the table. While still holding his hand Joanne sat next to him and said "I need to explain some things, but because of the way that went down you're already ahead of me. Like I said, you're for all practical purposes dead and I was assigned to find you. I'm like a counselor, your counselor."

Alex continued to say nothing out of both freight and anger, but Joanne proceeded with her assignment "Gee, where to start?" she said. The only response Alex could think of was "But I don't want to be dead. I can't be. Not me", he said in a way that demonstrated protest to the situation but he knew his stance could not last against what he had already observed. She took pity on the man and said, "It's okay to try and deny this. I did the first time I passed because it's only the natural thing to do." That only seemed to depress Alex even further and he briefly conceded with the question, "So what is it, heaven or hell for me?" She nodded with approval towards his question and said, "Okay, fair enough let me explain and few things. You are what we would refer to as a toss-up" Alex shook his head and wrinkled his forehead out of confusion and Joanne clarified by saying "When someone passes there are several different options, the most common three are heaven, hell, or your situation, a toss-up." Alex broke his stare and gazed off into the distance and said "Well when you put it that way I feel so much fucking better now, thank you so much" the sarcasm was undeniable.

Joanne said nothing but her glance at Alex said it all.
She was not in the mood to put up with a negative
attitude but also knew he would not go easily and she
lacked the strength to drag him. Alex let out a deep
breath and stared off into the vacant distance and said,
"Okay, so you're an angel and I'm a toss-up reject, I
guess this day couldn't get much worse." While still
holding his hand Joanne spoke up and said, "My dear
boy, you're missing what I'm saying and gravitating
towards the negative, you tend to do that. At least
that's what my research showed." She let out a slight
laugh before saying "First off, I'm not an angel, I'm a
counselor. There is a huge difference. You earn the roll
of a so called angel; it's something you work for
although we all report back to the same place. Over the
years mankind has done a really spectacular job of
messing up religions. Someone's always trying to
rewrite it to make it their own for control reasons. Even
these terms 'heaven', 'hell', and 'angel' are not quite
what you've been led to believe. Trust me humans are
way off on the soul and salvation thing. In the
meantime let's try and do away with these terms unless
really needed, it'll probably help clear your head." Again
Alex continued his silent puzzled expression and would
every so often look her in the eyes. "And yes your day
could have been much worse" she said knowing that
would get his attention. His eyes squinted and he asked

with more sarcasm "Oh really do tell 'counselor'. Is this where your way of screwing with me as we play out my own little version of 'It's a Wonderful Life'?"

This attitude was something she decided she would put up with for a little while as Joanne knew from experience that an array of emotions would be expressed in moments like this. Again she nodded her head and said, "You're not far from the truth, your fate is still being decided and yes, we will be working on it. And if you can't already tell I'm pulling for you." Joanne released her grip on the arm of her new client and stood putting her hands in her pockets. He felt the warmth of where her hand was and wondered why she was giving off heat for a being that wasn't alive in an earthly sense. "And by the way, that is a great movie and more on the spot than you realize" she said in a defensive manner. Alex broke his attention from the conversation and again stared out across a frozen scene in a neighborhood he knew all too well. For the first time he noticed a delivery truck that simple materialized out of nowhere, its brown boxy shape came into being without a sound and he found this disturbing. "When did that get here?" he asked as he stood and felt the need to walk towards it and physically touch the side.

Joanne kept a close eye on her subject as he walked the twenty feet towards the truck as she understood his need to explore the workings and limitations of his new environment. After reaching the brown package truck Alex extended his arm and his hand made contact with the vehicle and again he took notice of the surface temperature and texture before turning his head towards Joanne with a look of confusion. "While we have some time to spend together feel free to ask questions, I'm sure you have a few by now" she said as she began a leisurely walk towards Alex. As he stammered for his words and said "Uh, yeah I have a few" and began slapping the side of the truck and he continued by asking, "How come I can feel this? The heat on it, the surface, the texture?" The sound of the contact echoed inside and Joanne smiled as if she could not wait to share with him some secrets of this new existence.

"This is one of my favorite parts, the question answer portion", said Joanne as she leaned against the truck. Joanne looked around the still landscape and said, "First off there is a lot to explain, all of this physical world that you were a part of, you still very much are. The heat you feel is energy and the vibrations of it, and you are the energy once contained in your body, so thus you can feel it." "Goddamn!" exclaimed Alex as he slapped his hands against the truck as they produced a loud thud before walking away in disgust. "I was no saint, but I deserved better than this! This fucking is not right!" shouted a now visibly angry Alex. This change in temper was also something Joanne had dealt with in the past and knew it could quickly escalate unless she took immediate action. "It's okay to be angry and you can vent, but you must focus", she said as Joanne tugged on his sleeve before he pulled away.

For the first time he noticed some sort of physical dominance over her small stature and began plotting on how to exploit this observation. "How come I can feel when you try and move me like inside Robbie's bedroom?" asked Alex with his eyes locked on Joanne for her response then adding "Shouldn't you have all kinds of powers and shit like that?" The way Alex stared at her gave Joanne a strong suspicion that something was being planned in the mind of Alex but always being one for honesty she told the truth. "Higher ups have that sort of ability but I don't. You could say I have the strength of a one hundred and ten pound female, I'm not exactly a linebacker", she said as a hand was once again laid on the arm of Alex and once again he decided to further size up the situation by forcefully pulling away. By breaking free he then noticed the relaxed and caring expression on her face had now shifted to one of concern, she knew he was figuring certain things out as Alex smiled and asked, "What would happen if we arm wrestled?"

Silence settled between the two as he patiently awaited her answer and could see Joanne struggling with thoughts on the proper response. There was no doubt in her mind as to the point of his question and although she wouldn't admit to it she always felt bothered by her lack of physical strength in her last form of earthly existence. "You know I'm not here to arm wrestle with you, I'm here to keep an eye on you and to help you" she said with her confidence fading. Again displaying a sly smile Alex boldly asked, "So what if I ran?" as he readied himself. Joanne put up her hands to assure him that his mindset was very clouded and such a thought should be done away with. "Alex that's a really horrible idea, you can't even begin to understand just how bad" she answered as Alex allowed her to grab a hold of the sleeve of his shirt again before quickly pulling away. His own personal anger had now once again begun to spike and felt no need to conceal his feelings as he said, "You say it's okay to be angry? Lady that doesn't even begin to cover how I feel right now." His eyes shifted from left to right and his head turned in all directions as if to verify his location in this dilapidated section of town he knew like the back of his hand.

His legs tensed up and he made a quick lateral move before stopping, the look on the face of Joanne was now that of an anxious person knowing her options are greatly dissipating before her eyes. After one last judgment of the current conditions Alex said defiantly "I hope you understand that I can't just stand here while some sort of understudy keeps tabs on my ass while someone decides my fate, no way no how." Her arms fell limp at her side and she knew of his intensions and felt powerless to stop him. "Alex please don't" was uttered just as the young man began sprinting across the courtyard of the apartment complex. Joanne was quickly behind him giving chase and was astounded by the velocity of Alex, as hard as she tried she could not keep up with him as she was now over forty feet behind him "Alex! Don't!" screamed Joanne now realizing he would continue to increase his lead until he was nothing but a speck on the horizon and eventually be gone and lost in a world of risk that he didn't understand. As she came to a complete stop in the middle of a vacant and cracked sidewalk she realized that she needed to formulate a new plan and find her lost subject.

CHAPTER 5

Although his feet were bare against the pavement Alex had no problem in gaining speed and then completely leaving Joanne behind, but still not really sure what to expect he made sure not to rest easy and let his guard down. When he had reached a distance of at least ten blocks since he had last seen her he slowed his pace to a brisk jog and then to a walk. The familiar pains that would accompany running so far and so fast were not present and he felt as though he could keep up the pace for an indefinite amount of time and distance. Alex at this point was too interested in his surroundings to worry about Joanne finding him, and if she did he would simply run as he had done before. To him it was a simple solution to a simple problem. He noticed several parked cars and placed his hand on them to feel their presence as it was reassuring to him that he was still anchored to the world he once knew even if in a new and different way.

For the first time he noticed a raven perched high in a tree and was both curious and optimistic to find another living creature and. First and only thought was to make himself known to this bird shiny and black in the tree above. "Hey!" he screamed as loud as he could from the ground into the canopy of the birch as the bird indeed looked down to Alex below. Its head tilted and swiveled as it stared back in equal curiosity. Alex was pleased with the results so far and decided to push the experiment further as his picked up a small stone from the base of a nearby chain link fence. Taking aim at the black bird Alex heaved the rock upward into the tree and listened as it tore through the bare branches. The black bird quickly exited and began to fly parallel with the city street with Alex now being the one in pursuit. His only goal was to follow the bird and not let it escape his view, the pull it had on him was incredible. As he ran and began to wonder why it didn't ascend in altitude or break from its strict linear course.

Traveling swiftly and running with his head upward as to not take his eyes off of the creature he loved the idea of this bird beating against the very air to stay aloft. Every so often he would glance in front of him to take an assessment of the environment, once pleased that there were no obstacles his attention would return to the sky and the raven traveling thirty feet over his head. This pursuit lasted longer than Alex had anticipated and soon noticed the bird had developed a substantial lead and was now gaining altitude, but mysteriously remained in eyesight.

There was a sudden and unexpected stop in any forward motion as he had made contacted with a motionless car that seemed to come out of nowhere. There was no pain as Alex was thrown to the ground from being bounced off of the small older four-door sedan. Instead of searching the area for other vehicles Alex shot to his feet, his attention was back to the sky and he could see the raven had now left his sight, not even a sound to follow remained. "Damn" was the first word out of the mouth of Alex with his head still pointed upward while standing perfectly still and ready to bolt in any direction.

The sound of laughter now reached his ears and there was no doubt it was definitely a female as he feared Joanne had found him and Alex began to ready himself for another sprint towards freedom. As worried as he was that he had been located he noticed how intoxicating the sound was and after several turns had discovered the source sitting approximately twenty-five feet away. His first impression was how breathtaking her smile and beauty were. She sat on a park bench with her legs crossed and hands in her lap and was wearing a black ankle length skirt and a gray blouse. Her black hair was long and was draped over the back of the bench in wavy curls. Her complexion perfect and her skin had a healthy tan; to Alex she embodied every attractive feminine trait right down to her warm brown eyes. He stood frozen in his tracks and was scared to even speak as he felt this would disturb this perfect scene being played out before him. There was no denying that she too had her attention on Alex and this did raise several questions to him that he preferred to sweep aside and instead chose to concentrate on her beauty.

"Oh don't worry love, there will be other birds to chase", she said as he both tensed up and mentally relax at the sound of her voice. He now noticed she had a British accent which made her even more endearing to him and piqued his curiosity further. She motioned him closer with one free hand and said, "It's okay, I won't bite. Do come closer so we can chat." With an even greater attraction than with the raven Alex began to approach the woman seated on the bench, he still had his guard up but found that every attempt to resist her charms was a failing effort on his part. He managed to come to a complete stop fifteen feet from her and she said, "Still scared huh? That's okay. I know you've been through a lot today and it's only natural to feel off kilter." Once he gained the courage to speak Alex nervously stammered "Hi, I'm Alex." Her smile shown like a torch as she said, "Yes I know who you are, my name is Ashley and it's lovely to meet you Alex." She remained seated but extended a hand to shake and as drawn to her as Alex was for the time being chose to keep his distance. The sleeve on her arm slipped back to reveal a sliver bracelet to which Alex was even more endeared to her as this was his favorite metal.

She seemed a little insulted by the degree of caution that Alex displayed and said, "Sweetie, I'm here to help you. You can trust me." The tone of her voice rang like a song as she ran a free hand through her long shiny hair. "You'll have to forgive me Ashley, I sorry for acting this way" said Alex now smitten. Ashley cocked her head to the side and pulled a hand full of hair over her left shoulder and laughed flirtatiously before saying "You my dear have nothing to be sorry for, now how can I help you today?"

"Well I'm very lost right now, I have no idea where I am" said Alex shuffling his feet and breaking his stare on Ashley as he looked around. He had always prided himself on knowing the city very well, but he was at this point and time unable to recognize any buildings or read any street signs. Every sign that would normally indicate some clue to his location was altered and unreadable as the fonts were smudged and smeared beyond recognition. This observation upset Alex but his feelings were calmed by Ashley as she continued her small talk and urged him to come closer and have a seat beside her. Alex began walking in a wide circle around the bench where she sat, wanting desperately to join her but also still very shy about every move she made. "How can you help me?" asked Alex on his second lap around Ashley. She then laid on even more charm and replied, "Well perhaps you should tell me what you want, that would be a start."

The thought of having options halted Alex in front of the bench as Ashley still remained seated. Ashley winked "Ah, I see I have your attention now" she said pointing at him and grinning. True he liked the idea of options instead of being told things were being decided for him and asked "You mean I can decide what I want? You can do that for me?" "Yes I can Alex. I know what you've been through today. It's truly sad you were not given a choice earlier, but we can indeed fix that" said Ashley before adding, "Now come have a seat" as her lovely hand gently patted the empty spot next to her. Alex stood still as he took a moment to think about what he wanted out of this, or if he could change things what they would be. He also became a little more upset that Joanne had not given him such a choice. Then the answer became all too clear as he said, "You know, I do know what I want now." Ashley flashed her hypnotic smile and tilted her head again before saying, "See, making up your mind wasn't so difficult, now come over here and let's talk about it."

His left foot was the first to be picked up and motioned in the direction of the beautiful woman beckoning for him to join her on the bench followed by his right foot as she maintained constant eye contact. The sound of fluttering and running footsteps could be heard to the right of Alex but he found the gaze of Ashley too strong to break as she encouraged his movement, even requested he expedite his actions. Alex was on a course for the bench when he was hit hard from the right, the force was so great it knocked him from his feet and to the ground, the world now seemed ninety degrees off and he realized he was now on the ground and the look on Ashley's face was one of anger as her hands were now tightly gripping the bench where she sat. A new sensation soon occupied Alex, it was a crushing sensation and he realized he had a large man on top of him holding him down. As hard as he tried and struggled he could not break free.

"You stupid man!" was the first words said to Alex while he tried thrashing his elbows about to gain his freedom and make his way to the bench next to Ashley. He was so close, within ten feet. "You're not getting this one. He's ours and I'm taking him back!" said the voice now booming in his ears. The only feeling Alex could compare it to was holding a bug down and watching it squirm helplessly before he realized the one thing he wanted was slipping away. "Let me go!" demanded Alex before begging, "I need to go back! I want to go home! I want to go with her!" The voice of the man now said in a lower tone "No dice my friend. We have to get you out of here, you're in danger" as Alex was pulled to his feet, his stare still on Ashley who fought the urge to stand. "Ashley do something please!" begged Alex not wanting to break is attention from her.

Her head twisted from left and right frantically while shouting and asking, "Where are you? What are you waiting for? He's here!" over and over. A large arm encircled his chest and trapped his own arms as he was now being pulled kicking and screaming away from the bench and the salvation offered by Ashley. The harder he fought the more force was being used to subdue the weaker Alex. As the image of Ashley began to diminish in size her voice still stood out as she maintained making her previous statement "Where are you? Come on! He's here!"

"Why won't you help me?" asked Alex now over a block away. "Just shut up!" said the man that Alex still had not yet laid eyes on, but once far enough from Ashley he noticed his arm was large and muscular and that of an African-American. More begging ensued as Alex only wanted to be freed from the grip of his captor and return to the bench and to Ashley. Still not sure where he was he did know he was being pulled into an ally between to red brick buildings. A large hand grabbed him by the chest and forced him against the wall with a thud as dust shot out from behind him and for the first time he came face to face with the man that ruined his chances of having choices. "Just how stupid are you anyway? Oh no wait, don't answer that just yet. I heard what you did to your body." His eyes were dark and he had small pockets of gray hair in his tightly cropped haircut. As Alex began to down calm he noticed his attire was that of Joanne's but he didn't offer the same comforting manner as she did.

Alex fought the over powering man but to no avail as he said, "Please let me go, I need to go back." The temptation to join Ashley on the bench had now mushroomed and was now greater than any drug he had known and he felt the want to pursue that path could drive him insane, but it was a path he seemed more than willing to take. "Alex just calm down or we are not going to get along!" demanded the overpowering man clearly holding all of the advantages between the two. With every thrash and pull Alex could feel the fight in him subsiding, or at least he was realizing the futility of his efforts. Alex then sighed and put both hands on the thick arm of his keeper as he now came to the conclusion that he was indeed defeated as his eyes shifted back and forth and then sank to the ground out of shame.

"Okay now. My name is Nathan and you are one lucky son of a bitch", said the man pinning him to the wall. As Alex continued staring at the gray and broken asphalt at his feet he and was forced to utter "I don't understand any of this. Why? She was going to help me." "No Alex, no" said Nathan shaking his head and looking at Alex with the protective intensity before saying "She works for them, you were being duped." "Who?" asked Alex as he worked up the courage to look Nathan in the eyes. Showing less anger then he previously had Nathan slightly relaxed his grip on the chest of Alex and said "Well my friend if you had not run off like some fool and given Joanne a chance she could have explained this to you, when you hear us say 'them' we mean The Devil or Satan as you would refer to him in your Christian upbringing. Everyone has a different name I guess."

Alex couldn't help but doubt the statement just made by Nathan and challenged it by asking "And how do I

Ryan DeRome

know that you don't work for them?" but before Alex
could finish his question he found Nathan laughing.
"Boy if I worked for them then you would already be
there and when I say 'there' I mean hell, which is not
the lake of fire and Sulphur shit you people scare each
other with, it's much much worse." "I guess I don't
understand any of this at all, I mean she was so pretty
and she works for them?" asked Alex relishing the fact
that he was not being pressed against a wall. "Did you
ever read Homer?" asked Nathan "because it's just like
that, the singing sirens." The look on the face of Alex
told Nathan he was deep in thought before Nathan said
"Yeah she was pretty and sounded desirable, they know
what you like and will use it against you, she was like a
drug. In fact, I dare say she embodied everything you
would find attractive in the opposite sex correct?"

Alex had no choice but to agree and once again was
ashamed of his actions and became more in touch of
correcting his ways. Nathan placed his hands on his hips
and said "You're lucky I was able to find you when I did,
because a few more seconds would have made all the
difference." As the two men stood in the shadow the
buildings in a narrow ally Alex continued to struggle
with the events that had taken place and asked "If
Ashley was so evil then why didn't she just stand up and
take me?" "Very good question my friend, asking is
good" said Nathan now a bit more enjoyable now that
he wasn't holding Alex against a wall adding "Joanne

was just getting to this when you ran from her." The once abandoned Joanne would now be a welcome site and all Alex could think of is apologizing to her.

"It's all about energy, you, me, Joanna, Ashley, us, and them" said Nathan now taking a few steps back and raising his arms in the air. "Our souls, our energy, what leaves our bodies doesn't die, it's an imprint of who we were and are. You were physically stronger in your last life than Joanne, so your soul has that energy level and could run faster, thus you got away. Ashley was waiting on help to capture you, she couldn't do it with looks alone" said Nathan with the passion of a man giving a sermon. "So what about you and your 'imprint' as you say?" asked a much calmer Alex feeling like he truly should be grateful in the presence of Nathan. "Oh me?" quipped Nathan, "I was a running back in high school, spent four years in the army, then became a police officer for 15 years, so I can kick your ass all over eternity. But I always work within the bounds of rules, so only if it's needed" before laughing and slapping Alex on the chest.

Nathan once again looked around and this was when Alex noticed the sky had not changed, the clouds were still in the same position they were when he and Joanne exited the apartment and went outside as Nathan said,

Ryan DeRome

"So mister 'born and raised' in Chicago, care to show me how to get back to Joanne?" Although he didn't even begin to question how Nathan would know this about him Alex was given a lead of ten feet as his new captor followed him back into the street knowing he was making another point that Joanne needed to make in person. Alex didn't recognize any of the buildings or land marks. He had spent his entire existence in Chicago and there was no place he did not know; a little bit of distress sank in as he looked up at the street sign on the light pole. Instead of the usual black lettering on a white sign it was a blank field which was a more disturbing departure from the signs he noticed a short time ago. This was when Nathan saw the confusion from his recently acquired fugitive and said, "Yeah, it was happening, you were lost, I'll let Joanne explain that one, trust me it was your lucky day."

"Lucky?" asked Alex before voicing his opinion by saying "I can't wrap my head around that. I'm dead and to boot I'm some sort of reject that your side isn't sure they want." This was something Nathan had heard time and time again as he then explained to Alex that although things looked bad they could indeed be much worse, "We really need to get you back to Joanne" he said as Nathan now led the way confident that Alex had abandoned any thoughts of running. As the two men ventured down the street Alex kept scanning the scenery looking for any signs of the home he once

94

knew. "So you do the same thing Joanne does?" asked Alex in an attempted to fill the void where there was silence. "Yep" replied and upbeat Nathan before adding "We got into this line of work at the same time, had the same training group, so we just hit it off." The street signs still had not gained their names back but some structures were beginning to make sense and Alex was beginning to make out the shape of the skyline he had known his entire life as he said "I guess I missed a lot while goofing off in Sunday school, at least the few times I went" and as if he had a moment of clarity he added "I guess I should have paid attention."

"Well Alex if it makes you feel better I'll tell you that there is a lot about the existence beyond this world that simply isn't known until you spend some time here, but that's something that Joanne should really explain" said a smiling Nathan feeling that he was reaching Alex. "Once someone leaves their body it's up to us to find them and help them and make it back. Or we sit with and council them in the case of a toss-up. That's what Joanne and I do, it's our job" said Nathan. As the two walked there were spells of silence and Alex turned his thoughts to people that he knew would be left behind, he wasn't very close to his mother, but still his heart broke thinking about what her reaction would be to this news. But most of all he began to think of Samantha and what this would do to her, this was when he decided to distract his wandering mind with questions aimed at Nathan.

"So you were a cop?" inquired Alex as they both crossed a footbridge through a local park as yet more of the city began to look and feel familiar again. "Yes I was" answered Nathan, his reply was short and to the point, and this piqued the interest of Alex even more as he then asked "So, can I ask what happened? I mean how did you get here?" This question brought both men to a complete halt and Alex began to think twice about his friendly questioning. "I'm sorry, I can tell that question bothers you", he said. Nathan looked at the ground as Alex watched the smile disappear from his face "No, that's okay" he replied now staring off into the distance. He had a look of severe concentration before adding, "I know I was killed in a traffic accident on my way home from work, I honestly didn't feel a thing it was that fast."

Alex dared to not disturb Nathan as he could tell he was trying his best to remember as his eyes shifted back and forth. "This is weird because I haven't talked about it in so long" said Nathan shaking his head. "The woman that ran the red light, her name was Meredith. I was killed instantly and a man named Jacob came for me and said we couldn't leave until she made up her mind" said Nathan looking relieved that he could recall all of this then going on to say "And it was the most bizarre thing, I was angry and in a total panic and he was great at calming me down."

Nathan took a seat at the end of the bridge on a concrete step and said "Meredith would appear, and then disappear and then do it all over again several times. Her soul was going in and out of her body and Jacob gave her the choice, so she went with us." "Wow" was all Alex could say before Nathan continued his story with "It felt like I was at that accident scene for days, but it was only minutes. Man, I was so pissed off at her and Jacob made us all sit down and talk things out. The anger did take a long time to work through." Nathan now stood and looked at Alex and then said "Jacob explained to me that it was just an accident, nothing more. Accidents just happen, be it in a car, or being careless with drugs. Humans are pretty much left to their own devices and we more or less stay out of 99% of what's really going on." Although the command was unspoken the two proceeded with their walk back to Joanne and the mind of Alex became a buzz with more questions for Nathan and for Joanne once he made it back. He felt it best to use the time to reflect and prepare himself for his nearing reunion with her.

CHAPTER 6

A journey of more than three or four miles would normally tire the physical version of Alex but as the city became more recognizable he began to calculate the distance traveled to approximately six miles. This was a nice advantage to living in the same city his entire life, he could always look up and find his way, or at least most of the time still disturbed at how he became so easily lost. The haze that normally hung over and shrouded the skyline was characteristically different today. Instead of the average grayish white blur he normally saw that gave the buildings the appearance of being behind large sheets of vellum he was now being treated to various color spectrums not visible to the typical human eye. It didn't take Alex long to catch onto certain realities of his new existence and he didn't want to break the stillness and wonderment by questioning what he already knew to be truth. Instead he just enjoyed the light show and wondered how temporary all of this truly was and if he'd be able to enjoy such visions in his next stage of existence. The conversation with Nathan had long tapered off as Alex turned his thoughts to how he would apologize to Joanne and basically throw himself at the mercy of the jury. Throughout his life he could always convince people of the level of his sincerity, it was as if he had a gift for being on the defensive.

Every so often Alex would be amazed at a car materializing out of nowhere or on the opposite end of that steadily disappear into thin air. "Joanne did get to explain that, right? About seeing fractions of time and events?" asked Nathan as Alex stopped to put his hand on the fender of a red sports car and even though it appeared still he felt as if he could feel the engine working beneath the surface. "Yeah, she did get some of that out before I fucked up and ran," said Alex as the embarrassment was now dripping off of his voice before asking "How mad is she going to be at me?" as he traced his finger on the edge of the car in the street, he could barely make out the latent image of a young man in the driver's seat and was uneasy with this find. Nathan took note of the scene and explained that "You can see his energy, so you can see some of his physical existence, and he can more than likely see yours even if for only a second or so, but he's too busy to see you or if he could he wouldn't be able make heads or tails from it."

As if Alex had a moment of enlightenment with a stunned look on his face he turned to Nathan and asked, "So you're telling me that I'm a ghost to him like he is to me? Does that mean I'm partly physical? Can I communicate with him?" His questions were in quick secession and revealed the excitement in his voice, excitement that he hadn't felt in so long that it made him envious of the times in his life when this feeling was really quite normal, a much better time that felt so long ago. "Hey slow down. Yes he can see you but you left your physical self in that apartment. Listen Alex, it's hard to explain, it's both simple and so complicated it defies explanation, but I'm leaving that up to Joanne to try and explain. And to answer your other question, I have known Joanne a while, we help each other out from time to time. I've seen her pretty upset before, but she is the forgiving type so you've got that going for you", said Nathan. Alex did breathe a slight sigh of relief before Nathan tacked on "Then again, she's never dealt with a 'runner' before so it's an embarrassment in our line of work, not something we like to have happen."

"Yeah, I know, I'm real sorry about that" said Alex with the same amount of shame in his voice as before as he extended his arm and leaned against the red car looking into its interior, the chrome trim, the light brown leather seats, the fading man that seemed to be smiling as he himself was probably lost in thoughts only known to him. Alex then had a idea as he began to lightly tap the rolled up window that felt cold under his fingertips. "But what about my other question?" asked Alex focused on the driver in the car as Nathan knew what Alex was getting at, it was something he had faced often and for some reason he never liked delivering the news as he said "I know you want to communicate, everybody does but it's just beyond you my friend." Hearing this only made Alex more determined to make his presences known to the occupant of the car as he balled up his fist and began punching the window and the top of the car as hard as he could while yelling "I see you in there! I can see you! Look at me!" Over and over again this command was shouted while Alex wailed on the car like a fighter until Nathan shouted "Alex! Give it up man, it's not going to work! It never does."

The final three words seemed to take the fight and determination out of his mouth and arm as he could only ask "Why not?" Nathan reached out and gently guided Alex away from the vehicle as he said "That's the million-dollar question, everybody asks and nobody knows the answer, not on my level anyway. For some reason it's been one of the harder parts of my job, or at least what's hardest for me to help people with. I just like knowing that people can communicate, well when they are with each other." As Nathan spoke Alex noticed how far the two had gotten away from the car and back onto the sidewalk to continue the trek towards to Joanne. Not wanting to take that as an answer Alex said "There has to be away, there simply has to be." Both men were walking side by side as Nathan added "I feel you on that one, some say the secret is feeling connected to someone, but it's better to get the person on through the process rather than let them waste energy beating in the tops of cars and trying to scare people" and with that Nathan added a laugh and nudged Alex in a joking manner.

After yet more travel Alex could tell they were within two blocks of Robbie's place and even though Alex was aware of his lack of a physical stomach he still felt nervous and nauseous and had to question why this was the case to Nathan. "Just because you no longer have a stomach doesn't mean you can't feel that sensation of emotion. That only means you have a conscious, that's a good thing and there's hope for you yet. Emotion is in more places than your heart," answered Nathan. With every step the tension inside of Alex increased until finally the imaged of Joanne came into view as she was sitting at the picnic table from earlier. Without moving she watch the two men walk closer as Nathan brought the two to a complete stop while putting his hand on the chest of Alex and said, "You should stay here, I need to talk to her first" to which Alex replied "Sure, whatever will help." Alex then shifted his attention back to Joanne who was now standing and glaring at him with her arms crossed, she had the look of an angry school teacher and didn't break from her intensity as Nathan got further from Alex and closer to the upset woman that Alex abandoned in haste. When Nathan was within contact of her he put his right arm up and lightly turned her ninety degrees and hugged her, it was only then she broke the stare on Alex.

He felt voyeuristic as he watched the two have a conversation and catch up, but also felt disturbed knowing that a majority of the topic, if not all was about him. The brown delivery truck that had captivated him before his error in travel had begun to dissolve and in a steady moment was gone; it took his mind off of Nathan and Joanne but only made him think about the world now rolling on without him. Strangely he thought about his storage locker at work and how he had just hung up several pictures of people and places to remind him of more pleasant times when he wasn't pushing a broom. Or the apartment that he occupied and would never see again. Much like Robbie's place it wasn't in the best part of town, but he felt a real sense of home and calmness while there which was why he just signed another lease.

His legs weren't tired, but he still wanted to sit and feel grounded while he busied himself in more thought and reflection and settled on the curb. The street that he gazed upon was always busy and never as quiet as it was now, even at three in the morning there was always some activity and questionable at that. But there it was still and serene and for all purposes lifeless with the exception of the activity that he couldn't see taking place but still felt its vibrations. His focus on the peaceful void in front of him had grown very intense to the point that he did not hear the approaching footsteps of Nathan from behind. Once Alex detected the presence he jumped only slightly as Nathan took a seat beside him on the curb. "Still hanging in there?" asked Nathan now sitting on the ground. Not wanting to let this moment slip into irretrievable seriousness Alex put two fingers on his wrist and said "Yeah, I'm still dead." This longing for humor was something Nathan admired and replied "Well you're more alive than you think if you can still crack a joke in your present condition" then laughed and patted Alex on the back.

This was when Nathan noticed that Alex wasn't laughing and asked, "So, how mad is she?" Nathan was still smiling and said, "Well yeah she's mad, but she'll take you back. That's another thing I like about her, she doesn't give up on people." Nathan stood and faced Alex then extended his hand to help him up, once Alex was to his feet Nathan said "Remember when I told you about how it's an embarrassment to have a 'runner' in our line of work?" "Sure" answered Alex fighting the urge to look over his shoulder at Joanne in the distance as Nathan continued by saying "Well when we met and started training for this we both swore we'd always help each other with any runners. She's gotten one back for me, and I've recovered you for her. And don't think for a second that I won't help her." Alex was happy knowing that two people could be such good friends in this existence but when he began to show the smile on his face Nathan said "But listen up my friend. If I have to come and get you again or you step out of line it will not be pretty. Understand?" He felt as though he could do nothing but nod his head and look down as Nathan put his hand on his shoulder and said "Ok, let's go kiss and make up with Joanne" and led him over to where she was waiting.

The larger she became and the closer they got to her the more Alex could see her eyes burning holes in and through him. She stood with her back against a tree with her arms folded; she didn't need to speak because her body language said it all. Once within ten feet of her Alex spoke up and said "Hey I'm real sorry about that." At first he was proud of his forthrightness and assertiveness to admit his mistake until the long pause of silence sat in and he looked to Nathan for help as Joanne refused to break her stare. Nathan shrugged his shoulders and tensed his lower jaw muscles to express confusion before saying, "You're going to have to earn this one back."

"Earn what?" asked Alex.

"Trust. Respect. You name it you blew it buddy", said Joanne suddenly as Alex swung his head and full attention back towards her as she still had not removed herself from the tree. Alex straightened his posture hoping that would help him plead his case as he said, "I know I really screwed up, Nathan told me, I'm sorry." Her arms remained locked around her chest and she looked upon him as if in deep thought. As cross as she had been with him she wanted to make sure her words were chosen and delivered carefully, yet in a fashion that truly communicated the importance of the situation. "Like I said before you pulled this stunt, your case is up in the air. It's up to the both of us to show that what you have learned here in this life means more to you than the life you have led. So far your example is really poor", said Joanne.

He could clearly sense the disappointment she was projecting and Alex was once again confused and said "Joanne, with all due respect I don't follow what you're saying." "What she is telling you is that she is pulling for you, but she can't do it all, you have to prove it to Joanne and her higher ups. Even now your story and case is still being written" said Nathan in a more comforting tone of voice as he smiled at Joanne and said "Sorry, I know this one is yours." As some of this started to make sense to Alex he said, "Ok, so I'm being tested, reviewed. I'll step it up and pass" as his voice rang with optimism.

Joanne broke from the tree and said, "No, you just don't get it. As hard as you try to convince us that 'you get it', you simply don't. This life you had, that we had, can be such a simple and beautiful thing. But it's not about easy answers without substance." Nathan hesitated interrupting again but felt he should step in and said "Joanne only has so long to prove that you are worth another shot, or redemption." "Then what?" asked a blunt Alex with a more freighted look in his eyes. "You get turned over to them and there is nothing I can do to help after that", said Joanne as Alex could now sense the urgency and sincerity that she has towards his wellbeing and his future. More silence settled in as Alex absorbed what was presented as Nathan said "I really should let you two get to work, but first Joanna can I speak with you?" as he motioned her over.

She took several steps away from Alex and turned

towards him and said "I'm going to be right here, don't run" as Nathan then added "Oh trust me we had a talk about that." The feeling from earlier again coursed through him as he felt like a witness to a discussion about him however this time he was privy to crescendos in the conversation and every so often a word or phrase would rise above the two and make its way to Alex. Certain words such as 'helpless' or 'decision' seem to stand out to him as he both fought the urge to listen and yet gave into the need to pry for more information. This cycle repeated itself until the two broke from their meeting and approached Alex as Nathan then extended his hand and said "I'm getting this feeling I need to be in Schaumburg very soon, Alex I'm taking off, you listen to this girl because she's smart, she cares, and she has your best interest at heart." As Alex shook the hand of Nathan he knew that he was speaking the truth but also felt that he had barely scratched the surface with damage control towards Joanne. Then as quickly as the two had joined for a gentlemen's handshake the connection was broken and Nathan turned and began to walk away.

Once Nathan was a considerable distance away Joanne again locked her arms and returned to her stare at Alex as she had before and said, "They always said my first runner would be tough, but you have no idea. None at all." Alex spoke up to try and once again defend himself but was quickly cut off by Joanne. "No, don't speak, just listen" she said pointing at him to which he complied without hesitation. "All of my life I tried to help people. It was a short life, but I never stopped trying to be a good part of a larger picture." As if Alex knew she needed to vent and he knew he needed to accept this verbal lashing he remained quiet as she took several steps away and continued. "There is no way I can even get you to understand, and that's the sad part", said Joanne with her voice cracking.

Alex softly spoke up and said "Joanne, please just try and let me understand." She looked off into the distance down the road that Nathan had walked away on and to herself she wondered what it must be like to not have a care for others since she always had the benefits of others in mind. It was the way she was raised, but more importantly it was the way she was born and it was in her nature. Although highly unprofessional she continued in her assessment of Alex and their brief history and said "Even though I feel you are incapable of it, please think of a time you had your heart broken and multiply it by ten. Now think about how sad you have been, the lowest of the low points and multiply that by ten. Think of all of the saddest and most distressed events in your life and again, multiply by ten." Alex stood still and he ran through his own history in his head and thought about the truly sad and trying times that he had gone through.

By the look on his face Joanne could tell he was indeed giving much thought to what she said before she broke his concentration by saying "Because people like Nathan and myself, we're what are normally referred to as the 'sensitive types', but really we're like emotional antennas. That just prepares us for doing this if we chose to. We can sense things, and sometimes it's very intense, even overwhelming." A wave of shame passed over Alex as his head tilted towards the ground. This was when Joanne felt it best to lay in one last comment about his life and said "And you, what a selfish bastard you were, or should I say still are?" He knew he had this coming but said nothing as she continued "I fought every day for my existence; just to have one healthy day was amazing. People like you." Her tone had turned from sternness to bitter anger as she said, "People like you that have healthy bodies and throw it away. You had a good head on your shoulders and you didn't use it, you had a heart, but turned it off." She took several steps away and added, "I'm going to be over here calming down. If you want to run, then I guess that's your choice." He was stunned at her honesty and how she called the situation and his life for what it was. Alex wished he could speak, but somehow him dealing with the truth put so bluntly prevented him from voicing any thoughts what so ever.

"Okay" said Joanne "I think an important step is to almost begin from square one, but not quite all of the way because of time." Alex was silent and listened closely to Joanne and now looked upon her as if she were his last hope. The comfort from earlier had started to return to her voice and this also put Alex at ease for the time being. "Normally I would have been able to explain a lot of this new existence more in-depth, but well." As if he were clamoring to ask a question to help get the conversation going in the proper direction Alex inquired, "So what's up with these clothes anyway?"

Joanne put on her business face as she knew it was the act of a desperate man now realizing the assistance she could offer and said, "Yes, the clothes. Good question. Well the clothes have changed over time, you really would not want to be dressed in what was worn over 400 years ago or a toga so they somewhat match the time frame in which you pass." As she concluded her statement Alex noticed a clear and decisive change in her tone, the caring inflection from earlier was almost completely gone as if her enthusiasm for helping him had begun to evaporate. In an attempt to crack a joke Alex replied, "Yeah trust me, you don't want to see me in pantaloons or naked" before stopping his joke mid-thought. He placed a hand on his chest and felt a strange sensation deep inside of him. "Now what's wrong with me?" asked Alex with a confused look on his face. Joanne placed her hand on the shoulder of Alex and gripped tightly as he described the swirling feeling in his chest and how it seemed to push and pull towards the northwest, towards the apartment that contained his body.

She knew what this meant and also knew this created a different set of obstacles for her and Alex, ones that she lacked the mindset for at this point in their relationship as she was now questioning how much Alex even cared in the first place. This was also off set by her own fresh doubt in herself that she could impact and change Alex in time. "Joanne?" he said in distress that was fueled not only by the mood of the feeling, but the intensity of it and then said, "I'm a little worried now" and became silent. Realizing she had a job to accomplish and knowing that this doubt that has now arisen was probably just another test in a much larger plan Joanne said "Yeah, that's your body wanting you back, it has a little charge left in it, so to speak. The spark of life you could call it." "I need to see it again, just once more. I can't explain why. Please?" he begged. A few more cars began to fade into existence in the frozen landscape and this was when Alex could see the red lights on top of the several vehicles in the distance and knew one was an ambulance, the other appeared to be a police car. The fact that they appeared without a sound was not what bothered him, it was that he knew what they were there for. "Please Joanne?" begged Alex once more as she assessed the situation and observed Alex taking in the entire event from the sidelines.

"Do you feel like running again?" she asked as Alex was very truthful and ashamed in his response by saying "Yeah, and it scares me a lot. I'm so confused right now. I need to be up there, but the hell what would it solve?" Alex then began a tense pace back and forth with his eyes wide open but not concentrating on anything specific in his shifting field of vision. Joanne rubbed her forehead in thought and said to Alex "Calm down for a second, I think I have an idea." Hearing this he stopped in his tracks and put his hand back on his chest while giving all the attention he could muster towards Joanne. but not able to completely take his thoughts off of the feeling in his torso. "I need for you get to your knees and to close your eyes, I'll get you out of here" she requested of Alex as he watched her dropped to a kneeling position on the ground to which he quickly complied in front of her. His eyes were now tightly locked as he first felt the near presence of Joanne and then her hand on his eyes and said, "This may appear to be like a cheesy parlor trick, but no peeking." With his world in darkness he felt nothing but the warm hands on his eyes, the wind suddenly pick up where there was no hint of any before as the feeling in his chest subside to normal levels, or at least what they were.

CHAPTER 7

With her hands still over his eyes Alex noticed that had wind had subsided down and the smell of fresh cut wood now became apparent. He also noticed he was now kneeling on what felt like was a hardwood floor. "I brought to you to a place where you'll feel safe" said Joanne as she slowly pulled her hands away from the eyes and face of Alex. The location was no mystery to him as he asked in a voice of wonder "Oh my God, how did we get here?" Alex and Joanne were sitting on the floor of the tree house that he and his childhood Stan had constructed when they were eleven years of age. Everything was exactly as it was down to the last minute details. It was a perfect little box structure suspended twelve feet off of the ground in a catalpa tree located in the backyard of the of the house where Alex grew up.

As if Joanne were no longer present Alex began rubbing his hands across the floor as if looking for any proof of fraud in the little tree house. But it all fit together the way it always had in his memories, only better because this felt like the real thing. The crooked hinges on the trapdoor that exited down to a series of wooden planks nailed into the tree. Or the three near perfect squares cut out of the sides for widows that never had the covering built and left areas exposed to the elements. This was an item both he and Stan had intended to build, but never got around to once the tree house was functioning as a safe haven for two best friends. As he pulled the trapdoor open he noticed the squeak that always occurred just before it laid flat on the ground and then the rope and tire swing suspended under the floor on the main branch of the tree.

Alex then crawled over to the window that faced east and had the best view of the quaint house he spent his childhood in. From the tree house Alex could see the single story dwelling of white vinyl siding and gray shingles. The yard was very cramped and only had enough room for a small set of lawn chairs, an old grill that was beginning to show spots of rust, and the mature tree that Alex and Stan used to construct the tree house. As he looked down on the house Alex said, "I don't understand, this place doesn't exist anymore. This tree was struck by lightning when I was like sixteen, it all fell down." As soon as the statement left him he felt foolish for even asking or thinking about the 'how' and 'why' and decided to rest his chin on the edge of the window and just enjoy this moment. The unmotivated voice of Joanne spoke up and said "We're not in a place in the physical world; this is a place in time that'ss just near to you." As he continued his stare out at the world that he once knew he was amazed at how much he had forgotten. The worn out path from the screened back door to the base of the tree, or the faded orange Frisbee that was forever trapped on the roof after a careless throw. It always remained there out of touch, but not out of sight as it slowly lost its luster and became sun faded over the years.

"Stan and I had the best time building this", said Alex as though he needed to confess his connection with the tree house. His focus remained on the Frisbee as he told Joanne of how the both of them wanted to build this tree house but wanted to be independent and have as little help from Alex's dad as possible. "Stan could build circles around me", said Alex "he just had this skill it was crazy what that guy could make with Lego's and an Erector Set. He just lacked a dad at home I guess, you know, to do something like this. His mom was great and my mom and dad practically made him a member of the family, but he just grew up without a dad, that's all. His mom worked all the time to pay the bills." Alex rolled away from the window and laid flat on his back and from there looked towards the ceiling and noticed how the light would poke through the slats. Alex was now lost in thoughts of his childhood but more importantly of the tree house and Stan as he exclaimed, "This is when I was eleven and a half! Before we put the shingles on, I'm surprised we survived that stunt; my dad doesn't know how we risked our necks. We had to climb up onto the tree and work from there." As quickly as he had spoken up Alex became silent and still on the floor as now just thoughts of Stan remained in his head. From meeting in preschool and all of their social ups and downs in grade school and then high school they remained close until graduation.

Alex pushed away what sour memories he could feel gathering on the horizon and began slapping the floor with his hands and said in great exuberance "Wow, I can't believe I'm really here! I totally love this! Oh, by the way that was kind of cheesy with the closing of the eyes and the wind picking up." The giddiness inside of him was something he had not felt in years and to him it was the spark of being alive or being in love. In fact, these emotions were something Alex had not experienced in so long and had come to the conclusion that this was a feeling that he would no longer be privy too and the closest he could come was through the use of various drugs. The lack of action and input from Joanne now caught his attention as he propped himself up on his elbows and stared quietly at her as she in turned was looking at the world outside and apparently lost in thoughts of her own.

It took several minutes but once he built up his courage to speak he asked, "What's on your mind?" to a calm Joanne. She didn't break her gaze out of the window as she sighed and said, "It breaks my heart to say this but I think you might be a lost cause and all we have is this fragment of time." As the message was delivered and translated into thoughts and emotions, he had that all too familiar feeling of his adulthood, of someone giving up on him. Alex could not think of a single thing to say and lost track of how long the silence between him and Joanne had lasted until she spoke up again and said, "I never even got a chance to explain 'time' to you, I think you would have enjoyed it. It's not the constant that you think it is." As Joanne swung her head around to Alex she bypassed his face and instead concentrated on some candy wrappers in the corner and said, "I really miss the taste of candy" as her voice trailed off but never lost its sincerity as she added "Oh don't get me wrong, I miss my mom and dad, and my sister, and my cats, I miss them so much. I know it may sound strange, but I miss the whole candy experience too."

While listening he became slightly flush with panic that had swept over and settled on Alex as Joanne continued her brief reflection on candy as she reminisced and said

"It's not just the taste either, it was the picking out candy, all the choices, of trying something new or going with a favorite. And the anticipation of unwrapping and how you just knew it was worth any wait." He was still speechless and alarmed by her earlier proclamation of the dire prediction of him and yet she still insisted on speaking more on her love of candy. As she sat on the wooden floor she now shifted herself to face Alex head on but he only now stared down at the floor in apparent despair. Joanne felt as though she needed to engage him in conversation and said "What can you tell me about those wrappers? You must remember something about them?" Alex became indignant to her line of questions and felt he had no choice but to become short with his retort and replied, "I'm going to 'hell' and you want me to think long and hard about candy wrappers? No thanks, fuck that."

"I don't know why, but for some reason you need to remember, I need for you to talk about these wrappers," she said "Humor me". Alex sarcastically threw his hands into the air and yelled "Sure! Why not spend my little time left talking about faded paper in the corner? Gee that looks like Laffy Taffy to me, Inspector Alex is on the case." As he rolled his eyes with his response he crossed from one degree of emotion to the other and became motionless and quiet. His gaze was now locked on the wrappers and he said nothing but just looked at them with great intensity. "I can remember Stan loved those, they were his favorite" said Alex in a mutter that could barely be described as audible. He slowly sat up and pulled his knees to his chest, rested his chin on his right knee and then said, "We would buy that candy with any spare change we could find. First we'd go to his place and turn the cushions on the couch over, then onto my place; some areas were just goldmines for us. Sometimes the hunt for the change was just as good as the candy. My dad's car was always a sure bet; you know how change gets in the seat or under it." Joanne too had a soft focus to her eyes and slowly nodded her head and whispered "Yeah, I've done that too" as a small grim emerged on her face as she then said, "Even finding a wrapper blowing in the wind could totally change your day. Or even finding some untouched stashed away in your pocket."

With this last statement Alex jerked his head towards Joanne and said, "Wait a second, you were there today weren't you? As I waited for the bus?" Now it was Joanne that returned the stare of intensity and replied "Yes. Yes I was Alex. I got there about the same time you did." With this new information Alex snapped at Joanne "What? You were there? You fucking knew I was going to die didn't you?" as he slapped the floor in outrage and banged his head on the wooden wall behind him. Joanne could see his anger building and expressed and began to sense in herself feeling an overwhelming pity for Alex, not only for his situation and almost certain fate, but for her failing him. She crawled the short distance across the floor and put her hand on his hand, which was flat on the floor in an attempt to comfort him. "I may as well run again", said Alex "since I'm pretty much screwed anyway." As she squeezed his hand she felt the pressure of his in return as she said, "Listen, you're still with me, and that's a good sign." "Why did you let this happen to me? You could have stopped it", charged Alex now becoming even more emotional as if the idea of someone intervening was his breaking point.

"Listen" said Joanne wanting to gain control of the situation as she went on to say "I didn't know you were going to die. I was sent to you, like I've been sent to others and all I can say is that I have no direct control over what happens. All I can do is subtly influence the events and sometimes I have to be creative. Sometimes I have very little to work with." He began a long stare into her eyes in a manner of doubt as she then said, "And sometimes people pass, sometimes they don't. The need inside of you was just stronger than my hints and suggestions." Alex closed his eyes and thought hard about the day he had at work and the conversation at the bus stop with Donald and asked "I don't understand what you did to try and stop this?" As Alex remained tightly balled up with his knees in his chest Joanne sat in a more lounged position in front of him while not breaking her contact and said "Okay, I need to explain some things. As we go through life we have free will and the ability to make choices. Do you understand?" Alex was a still as a stone and Joanne said "You're a smart guy, so I'll take your silence as a 'yes' that you understand. So we have choices, but when your number is up, it's just up. It's in everyone to try and survive, but poor choices and time can be our biggest enemies."

A small bird landed on a branch on the tree outside of the window and Alex was startled at its presence. Instead of materializing and fading as other things had done this creature looked very real, so much so that Alex asked "How come that just appeared? The last bird I saw almost got me in trouble. Besides I thought time had slowed down or something like that." This bird was a welcome distraction from the tension that had grown in the last few minutes and she was happy to answer his question. "Right now we are in a moment in time that has passed; it was just safer to take you here. Time is progressing as it normally would here. When you first passed you noticed time was normal, right?" asked Joanne. "Yeah, now that you mention it" said Alex before simply asking, "Why is that?" Joanne flashed a smile, she was relieved that Alex was asking questions with a concern to his voice and she said, "This is strange but follow along. Remember when we went outside and how everything slowed way down to beyond a crawl?" Again Alex nodded his head to agree as he now remembered and showed more attention to what

Joanne was saying. "The closer we are to our bodies or to loved ones the more normal time is, it retains its march forward" she said "Our bodies act like an anchor to the physical world and you're still trying to connect with your 'old self' so to speak." "Really?" was all Alex could ask as he was now in a sense of wonder at this information and he thought briefly how this concept reminded him of a rubber band. This pleased Joanne and she said, "Time in the physical world is a cadence. It's a rhythm that doesn't change. But in our current existence it ebbs and flows, it's very elastic. This is a good thing if you can handle it, which is why I'm glad Nathan found you."

As Alex stared at the black pants he was wearing and began to feel slightly ashamed as Joanne felt this change in his mood and said "You see, people that run can become lost out there. Then they become for lack of a better term ghosts. Trust me, it's not cool like in the movies, you simply exist in a state of confusion wondering why you can contact anybody. You can't go forward, and you can't go backwards. You are simply stuck." Again Alex trained his eyes on the bird outside of his window and for the first time in too long was grateful to watch this creature resting on the branch as Joanne continued her verbal lessons on existence and the world beyond the physical realm.

"So if a person runs and gets lost and neither side can reach them, sure they're stuck, but it seems better than hell" said Alex before adding "Not that I'm thinking of running again, but if you're telling me that's a better option I can take a hint." She could detect the sincerity in his voice and knew running was not in his intentions, but he was genuinely curious as she responded "If you stay out there long enough then you become unreachable to both sides, meaning they can't claim you. However they tend to like to find those who become lost and torment them. Since they can't really have you they will still try their hardest to make your life a living hell, again for lack of a better term. They are relentless."

Listening closely Alex extended the index fingers on his left and right hand and raised them as not to interrupt Joanne, but show them as a sign that he understood what she was telling him. "So, the other side can't have you but still get their jollies but making your existence hell", said Alex with his eyes perked up. As Joanne smiled she silently nodded her head in approval not only in his ability to figure out this most simple of afterlife fact but at how he took great pride in doing so. The feeling of intellectual victory was short lived as Alex still couldn't shake the impending feeling of doom from his mind as he asked "So Joanne, what happens to me now? I have a feeling you just can't leave me here in a tree house for eternity." "Yeah, that's the big question right now" she replied, "I need to figure out what to do with you, or how I can get more time with you." Both shared a brief laugh when the expression of 'time' came into play but soon both were quiet and deep in thought as of what their next move should or could be. Joanne tried to fall back on her training as they had told her to do in such circumstances, but nothing felt right to her, it was as if every decision would be wrong and lead to his damnation.

Alex was the first to speak up when he said, "Ok, I'm supposed to have an understanding of what this life was all about. So maybe we could just start from square one." As much as Joanne would love to take this route, she couldn't as she explained, "I only have so long to get you to see the point, then I have to turn you over to my managers." "Whoa, what? Managers? You have managers?" asked Alex in disbelief. As she sighed Joanne said, "Yes. I have managers. People above me that make sure I'm doing my job. This soul thing isn't totally automated you know." "But what happens if you don't check in?" asked Alex thinking he was coming up with a solution. As Joanne shook her head she said, "That's no good, if I don't find them then they find me. It's like a mark against me and I have a clean record." The desperation once again began to show in his voice as he said "So fuck the perfect score and make me a fugitive so we can figure this shit out, please Joanne." This statement did put certain thoughts in motion as she reflected on how she was always a perfect student and a stickler for the rules in her life. Rules gave her structure and boundaries that served as a guide, and she liked to think they helped develop her into the person she was.

"I'm not getting a warm fuzzy over here" said Alex displaying the most honest eyes he could. "I don't think you realize what you are asking me to do, this is a very big deal mister", she said trying to figure out the best way to let him down gently "This would go on my record and is against the rules. Big time." Alex continued his stare at Joanne and asked "What's more important, rules or a soul?" The question was posed and muted both parties involved in the debate, Alex was stunned at his last minute ability to come up with the question and Joanne was marveling at how the inquiry was short in size, but heavy in meaning. This was when Joanne came to the conclusion that training and being an astute pupil can't prepare you for everything and she had to rise to the occasion for herself and Alex and said "We need to buy more time, so we should keep moving." Hearing this excited Alex as he said, "Sure! Hey another safe place would be this bar on 11th street, I always had luck there" but could tell his weak attempt at humor was falling short as Joanne quickly cupped her hands over his eyes and the wind picked up once more.

CHAPTER 8

Gina sat on the couch sobbing and still shaking from what she had witnessed moments before. She realized that although she had seen worse acts of brutality in her short life the scene of Alex on the ground lifeless and as pail as porcelain particularly shook her soul. She secretly liked how he was an honest and nice person, which was something this world was always in short supply of and now having one less in its ranks. Tracing her fingers over the rough and worn material of the couch she quickly came to the conclusion that this was a terrible distraction from the reality at hand and knew some sort of small outburst was coming. "What are we going to do?" she asked of Robbie who was clearly under pressure as to what his next move should be and knew he didn't need Gina pressing him on any issues at this particular time.

He did his best to ignore the crying of Gina as he wandered into the kitchen to survey less disarray than what was in the living room area. The table that sat in front of him appeared lonely and he thought for a second of how he and Alex became friends over a game of cards at that very location. For reasons unknown to him he could clearly remember that evening and how Alex was invited by a friend of a friend and that the pot he brought to the card game was of particularly low quality. Robbie used that to hassle the new stranger all evening the whole time adding lines like "You should run with me sometime, I can get some good shit." And this gave him a pause at how prophetic this statement was. Every little detail came back to Robbie and began to haunt the man like an eerie sound that only he could detect and with every second became louder and louder until he was sure that either he or it would reach a breaking point.

With this torment hanging over him Robbie couldn't recall the last time he really thought about his life and the path he had placed himself on. Although he would never admit to putting himself in such dire straits instead Robbie chose to blame the world at large for being unfair and disingenuous to people like him. It was just easier that way, much easier than being responsible. Even from his vantage point in the kitchen he still heard the crying of his female companion and it infuriated him. "God dammit Gina, knock it off! Fuck!

I'm trying to think in here!" he shouted but to no avail as this only drove her emotion outpour to greater levels.

"Fuck" he them mumbled as he lightly punched his hips and turned in frustration to the other room. She was standing and wiping her eyes with her hands as a purse hung over her right shoulder. This was a clear indication that she was planning on leaving and Robbie greatly feared being alone. He didn't understand why he felt this way, after all it was in the kitchen that he found some solitary moments and it gave him a few seconds to pool his thoughts or at least try. "I can't stay here anymore, not today", she said with her nose sniffling. She only took two strides towards the door as Robbie kindly yet forcefully stopped her exit by grabbing her arms. "Stop" he said, "This is really fucked up, but leaving won't help anybody, I'll deal with the paramedics and whoever else shows up. I need for you to be cool okay?"

This bothered Gina as she looked at him in a phase of disbelief and confusion. Robbie too took a moment to note the heavy running makeup and lines under her eyes. They were more pronounced than what he had ever remember seeing them and wondered for a second if they were always like this. Even though she had been crying and her eyes were bloodshot he knew this was more than likely normal for her. "Yeah, because this is all about you now isn't it?" she said tensing up and expecting to be struck for her question and tone but continued in her brief speech. "Did you feel how limp he was? Did you? I did", said Gina before once again crying and leaving Robbie without words to mute her staggered breathing. "God I just want to leave", she said now covering her eyes and once again resting on the couch. Sitting still gave her time to reflect as Robbie quietly exited the small room. Gina thought of how she just wanted to be at home with Victoria and how takeout food and a movie sounded so simple and perfect as the situation suffocated her thoughts. If she had only stayed she could have avoided this, these unpleasant scenes and tension as she looked towards the bedroom where Alex lay lifeless. She put her arms tightly around her mid-section and began rocking herself slowly back and forth in a comforting manner as her mind wandered.

At first she tried to fool herself into thinking that if she had chosen not to come over to Robbie's place then none of this would have happened, then it occurred to her that she didn't buy the drugs or mix them, and lastly didn't put the needle in his arm. This line of logic was short lived as eventually she realized that this tragedy was probably going to happen whether or not she was present or having a quiet evening with Victoria. Gina then thought about how her and Robbie met and for the life of her couldn't recall any of the details or even the broader memories. It was as if he were always there even though their history was very short. The attraction was what motivated her last ill navigated relationship and the one before, and more than likely the ones to follow. Even though she could not recall how they began, she was beginning to see the darker side of how they might end.

"Gina" said Robbie from the kitchen as she could see his shadow pacing back and forth. "What Robbie, what do you want now?" she asked as his pacing and shadow stopped as he replied "I just needed to ask one more time if you got rid of everything, I don't feel like going to jail and having my life all fucked up from this." "Yes I got it all, Jesus Christ listen to yourself" she said realizing that the words will get through to him, but not the emotion and inflection. A curiosity then arose in Gina as she stood and walked towards the kitchen with her knees feeling weak and unsure with each step. There she found Robbie leaning against the dingy white kitchen cabinets with his head down in silence and she hoped he too was having a reflective moment. With her defenses down her heart began to go out for this misguided man that had the appearance of a lost boy in this light as she asked "What if it was me in there? What would you do?" This question broke what little stillness and clarity that had somehow assembled itself as

Robbie looked up and asked "Gina, what the fuck does that mean?"

He was sporting the look of a killer, his eyes half closed, his lower jaw tense with the veins in his neck pronounced. Every ounce of his glare was intended for Gina, to be silenced and more importantly to overpower her as he said "I'd do what I'd have to do" as his head once again slumped down towards the floor. In the distance both could hear the roar of sirens over the normal clamor of the city. It wasn't an unusual sound for either but both knew of the purpose and destination. Robbie then raised his head and looked off into the distance and said, "Here they come, so put on your game face" as he turned his attention back to Gina and asked if she had a cigarette he could bum.

The culmination of the previous statements and the calmly asking for a cigarette was too much as she spun in frustration, walked back into the living room and sat on the couch as she mumbled "Go to hell". The feeling to leave had receded if only a little but still gave her enough leeway to think things out a little more as Robbie stormed back into the living room expecting to find her attempting to exit once more. The sirens outside only grew in volume as they approached which only helped to ramp up the tension in the small apartment as Robbie said, "I know there's going to be an ambulance and maybe a couple of pigs, so just let me do the talking. If the cops want to question us separately then you don't know him, you've never met him, clear on that?" Robbie asked as he then walked towards the door and unlocked the deadbolt and then opened the door while still placing himself between Gina and the outside world.

Gina once again sat rocking back and forth choosing to say nothing as she felt as the need to run past Robbie and down the stairs, from there the courtyard would provide a nice open expanse to either widen any lead or make a scene to cause a distraction. Instead she made the decision to remain seated as she could feel Robbie staring at her and then to the outside world as the ambulance came to a halt on the street followed by a police car. With the door open the sound within the little apartment was piercing until the officers and paramedics muted the sirens but left the lights spinning to make all aware of their presence.

CHAPTER 9

As the wind subsided the first things Alex noticed was the strong sweet aroma of more wildflowers and the warm weather on his back with a light breeze passing by him like an invisible hand brushing his rather bland standard issue clothing. Joanne removed her hand from his eyes as he discovered that both of them were standing in a large open field in a rural area unknown to Alex. The patch of land stretched for at least ten acres and had random areas occupied by small forested patches with various wildflowers covering every square inch making them thick in density and almost waist high. The sky was the most perfect blue Alex had ever scene with white clouds sculpted in amazing organic shapes that defied logic. Being a city dweller all of his life left him envious of settings like this and knew it was something that you didn't appreciate until you saw it in person or in a situation as this. The greens were relaxing and ranged from muted to vibrate with a mixture of lavender and white daisies as some areas seemed too beautiful to be real and he questioned if this could ever really exist on earth.

"This should buy us a little buffer to try and come up with a solution" said Joanne trying to be a realist as she took note of how this field sent Alex into a trance as his eyes took in every shade of color the field had to offer. She too enjoyed this place and loved how Alex didn't need to speak to show his appreciation and admiration. Under his feet his could feel how the ground was slightly uneven as the growth around him had pushed the dirt in different directions in their geotropic stretch to the sun. "Wow" said Alex "Talk about being cramped up in the city too long, this place is beyond words." "Yeah I know, I decided to take you to a place that I love" she said as he wandered fifteen feet away and she felt comfortable in her judgment that he would not run. Joanne began to ask opened ended questions of Alex in an attempted to jump start her own thought process as Alex spun around and said "What is this place? Did you make all of this up?"

Trusting her instinct Joanne decided she needed to barter with Alex as she said "I'll make a deal with you, how about I tell you about this place and you tell me about those dog tags you were making a big deal about earlier. You don't seem the military type to me." Hearing this request made Alex sigh defensively as he said "I'm not" before a long pause then added "Listen, it's just history and won't change a thing, especially now" as Alex dropped to the ground pushing aside the stems, leaves, and flowers as he rested on the ground. He was hoping this would somehow shield him from any further questions and knew his options for hiding were very limited so he went with what seemed like the easiest and most natural thing to do. This course of action obviously wasn't going to work as Joanne walked over and settled on the ground next to him and said, "So what, are you just going to wait it out? I don't know why but for some reason it seemed like a good place to start a conversation."

He knew she was correct in her motives but he lacked the courage to talk about the dog tags he sorely missed and yearned for even in his state of limbo. The way the small metal plates felt against him as his heart would beat behind them within his chest. Feeling dazed Alex tried to say something but only stuttered and stammered. His poor attempt to construct words was futile as his ability to speak suddenly left him and could do little but stare at the ground as the moments of silence kept building on each other one by one creating a long pause. Coming to the conclusion that this was going nowhere Joanne said, "Ok, I'll start this", the tone of her voice was motherly or at least that of an over protective older sister as Alex was quick to respond, "Just because you want to talk doesn't mean I'll cave." "Yeah, but it's a risk I'll take" she said with a slight smile beginning to feel more like her old self, the one with a purpose.

"This place is close to where I lived with my family, I had it pretty good, never a lot of money but things were just good. No Great. Plus, I had my best friends close by" Joanne said, but was seeing how this introduction and back-story to the current landscape was not affecting Alex in the least. He instead began pushing at the dirt with his index finger and watched the soft brown ground alter and change with each poke. "Right now it's about 12:15 in the afternoon in early September. The weather was somewhat cool today, really just perfect", she said as he continued his exploration of the ground. Not that she was an inpatient person but Joanne felt a need to push her point and said "Come on Alex, stand up for a second because I want you to see this with me" as she rose to her feet and offered a free hand to Alex which he excepted but internally fought the urge, but still he lumbered to his feet.

Joanne pointed to the east and said "Out there is a road, you can't see it but it's there, the two fields so close together disguise it." She folded her arms and stared intently as she went quiet and waited. Her projection was that of a sentiment that Alex had trouble identifying with as her blue eyes remained focused on the area that she claimed a road to be. Breaking the mood Alex spoke up and said, "I don't see what this is" before Joanne put her finger to her mouth to indicate to Alex that he needed to be quiet as a small four door car with metallic green paint came into view. "There it is" said Joanne quietly in a voice barely above a whisper that was really only meant for her but Alex being in such close quarters heard clearly but chose not to ask any questions.

From their vantage point of about fifty yards the car appeared no larger than a toy as it gave away the location of the road that Joanne had alluded to and kicked up a light dust plum behind it as it began to slow and pull over. Without saying a word Alex took his attention off of the car nearly stopped and observed Joanne, knowing she was being watched she leaned over towards Alex and said "This is pretty cool, just watch." The car now at a complete stop at the side of the road as the passenger side door was quickly opened and a young blonde girl emerged with a large camera in hand. For a second Alex forgot about his current state and felt the need to duck into the wildflowers before shaking his head in silent embarrassment. The wind tossed her long hair as he could barely make out the girl saying, "This is perfect!" as she began adjusting the old camera with both hands. The driver's side door was slower to open as Alex could only make out a general outline of the person and it didn't help that he and Joanne were on the opposite side. But now with the driver now fully exited from the car she stretched her arms towards the sky, this was when Alex felt the need to walk closer to observe, even if it were only twenty more feet. As he began to walk as Joanne followed closely.

The short stroll did improve the point of view as now Alex could see the driver was wearing a blue shirt advertising the band 'R.E.M.' and she too was having her shorter hair tossed in the wind as the girl with the longer hair pointed towards the field and said "That shot would be awesome!" The girl driving the car then set foot into the field and gave Alex a clear view of her face to which he spun around in amazement and asked "I don't understand, is that your sister?" Although he only looked back at Joanne for a mere second he had time to see perhaps the largest most honest smiles he had ever seen as she said "Yeah, the one with the camera, the other one is me." Alex didn't know what to say or how to act as nothing in his life had prepared him to see something like this as his head quickly swiveled back and forth from the two girls by the road to Joanne standing two feet away.

She knew he was comparing her and the two girls and couldn't find anything physically out of place as indeed Joanne stood beside him and was also appearing about twenty yards away with her back now to the both of them. He couldn't hear the shutter of the camera but knew from the various poses that images were being recorded as Joanne would stand still in the distance and repeat the process changing her stance only slightly every five or six seconds. "This ought to freak you out", said Joanna laughing as she added, "Now you're kind of in a picture of me with me. Don't worry, we won't show up. Kodak made good film back then, but not that good. We're there in spirit anyway."

Soon both girls were back in the car and pulling way as Alex felt the need to ask, "Is this some kind of trick? How did that just happen?" "No, no tricks here" she said still beaming, "I just took you somewhere that meant something to me." As she watched Alex process what had just occurred she chose to not pursue the subject of the dog tags but instead offered her life up like an open book which was something she didn't make a normal practice of doing "Feel free to ask me anything you want" she said shrugging her shoulders. With a perplexed look on his face Alex said "Well gee, I guess my first questions are what did I just see and why did we come here?" Nodding her head Joanne replied "I was on my way home from going to the store with my little sister and the day was perfect, just like this. My sister was starting to study photography and she was looking for a place to take a picture of me." Alex kept listening as Joanne started to slowly spin as she kept talking and said, "I never said anything, but for about a week leading up to that day I felt something was about to happen and I had that feeling for the next two weeks, it just wouldn't go away and kept growing until something did happen. But for some reason I was just so darned happy that day and it showed."

Knowing that this first answer opened the door to a multitude of questions Alex cautiously asked, "Um, what happened? I mean to you. I take it that's where you're going with this" as he slowly leaned towards her not sure if his simple question went too far. Joanne spun around to face Alex and said, "Well, the short version is I passed away, or moved on about five or six weeks after this." Little in her line of work did Joanne ever mention her history even though she had made peace with it long ago and saw no harm in putting Alex in the know. Although she didn't forget the fact that she would soon have to turn him over, this place brought more relief as did the tree house and she could see the change in his attitude. "Well I was short of being twenty-seven when I left, or died, however you want to say it" said Joanne as she knew she had his full attention and continued "I had a bum ticker and was on

141

the transplant list, for quite a while really. They said I wouldn't last more than a year, but I showed them, I went twenty-two months waiting." "So you died waiting?" asked Alex hesitant to use such words as 'die' or any other death related vocabulary in her presence. "Oh no, I got it", she said "So never let them tell you that you can't do something, because when they do that means you can just prove them wrong."

Sensing that he still wanted to know more Joanne continued as she signaled him to walk beside her as to retreat from the road and into the field and said "Well needless to say it didn't take but sometimes life is like that." Confused by this Alex asked for clarification to which Joanne said, "My body rejected it, but I put up a good fight that I'm still proud of." They slowly walked and Joanne decided to add more details of her experience since she had a very captive audience. "I was in that hospital for almost a month, the ICU. And I started getting this visitor by the name Jacob. The problem was I didn't know anyone named Jacob. He was an older guy, kind of skinny with whitish hair. At first I thought it was strange that I could only communicate to him and not the nurses and after a while I thought he was a result of all the crazy drugs they had me on. I knew I had a tube in my throat so talking was out of the question, but I didn't realize this until after we had a few conversations and then it dawned on me. Those were some strong painkillers."

By now both had reached the place where they had both appeared in the field as Alex looked down and found his finger holes in the dirt from earlier as Joanne said "I guess hindsight is twenty/twenty because he was wearing the same type of close that I have on now, white pants and a tan sweatshirt." "Were you scared?" asked Alex as he searched for pockets to put his hands in and after not finding any he rested them on his hips. "Now really why would you have pockets?" asked Joanne followed by a warm laugh. Feeling foolish Alex too laughed and said "Out of habit I guess."

"So yeah, about Jacob" she said getting back to the subject at hand "He was sent for me but knew I wasn't wanting to leave since I was a fighter and had a lot to stick around for. Every time he would visit I learned more about him and what he did, so I guess you could say he influenced me to do what I'm doing now." Alex felt the need to ask an uncomfortable question "Did he influence you to let go, you know, not go on?" Joanne extended her lower lip slightly and turned her head back and forth as she said "No, oh no, he and I knew I wanted to stick around. He was pulling for me like everyone else was." Alex was relieved that she was okay with this question as he felt more questions like that could present themselves.

"About a week before I died I did 'step out' for a couple of seconds", she said as Alex hung on her every word and was now grateful to be an audience to Joanne. "I don't follow, what do you mean you stepped out?" he asked as she told him of how her transplanted heart had suddenly stopped "I just appeared from nowhere in the hallway outside of my ICU room, so I must have been asleep when it conked out. Jacob was right by me and ushered me away because he said it was best if I didn't watch them work on me. He was probably right, what I did see was pretty scary with all of the alarms going off and people running in. I told him I wanted to see my mom and dad because they were staying down the hall in what the hospital called 'a quiet room'. My family set up camp in there; really a cramped little room but they made the best of it." Joanne wrinkled her forehead and paused for a second as she was orchestrating her words and recovering her memories of the final phases of her last life on earth. She realized how lately she was really caught up in her line of work and hadn't stopped to think and remember certain events.

"Are you okay?" asked Alex concerned over the sudden stop in her recollection of events as she answered, "Yeah, I'm okay. It's just strange how I can remember what happened when I got to my mom and dad in that little room. Jacob and I had just gotten there and a nurse opened the door then turned on the lights and woke them up by telling them I was flat lining and a team was working on me. What a crappy way to wake someone up right?" Alex nodded his head as she continued by saying "The nurse sat there with my mom and dad and things got weirder, but my mom got this look on her face like she could tell I was there, she sensed my presence. Then she said in a voice that only a mom could produce 'Joanne get back in there and fight' so I did." Alex now had a very wide-eyed look on his face as she then said "But what was strange was right after she said that I had the same feeling inside of me that you had earlier, that pulling in your chest. I could feel that when it hit you, except mine was like being knocked over by a car."

"Were you pissed that you died? You know, for good." he asked again unsure about his tone as she could sense his hesitance and assured him by saying "What I felt was way too complicated to sum up with one word, it was a whole gambit of feelings. Sure there was anger and resistance, but I also felt love and gratitude, relief. Really the hardest part was knowing that everyone I was leaving would have a tough time with it. I wanted to tell them that I was okay and I didn't hurt anymore. Jacob was able to let me stick around for a brief time to be close to them and so they could be close to me. It happens when we have a strong bond people, they can just feel you. Saying goodbye helped a lot, I know they could tell when I was around in some form or another." Joanne again paused and rubbed the back of her neck as she stared at the ground and then said, "Over time almost everyone made some sort of peace with it. Well, almost everyone that is. It's just hard when you have a void in your life where a person used to be."

Alex began thinking about those he was close to both recently and throughout his life, the bonds he had made and foolishly broken. Or the friendships he had made and never kept up his end of the deal, or the brief love affairs that he had enjoyed but had tossed away thinking they could easily be recovered or replaced. His thoughts turned to Samantha as he began to wonder what she might be doing now. Perhaps she was standing in front of her easel in the spare bedroom of her apartment that served as her studio adding paint to canvas. She could be at the small bookstore three blocks from her place leafing through another book on Richard Diebenkorn or Gustav Klimt. This is when he began to feel ashamed of himself for not being stronger than his urges and wondered why the chemicals we put into our bodies can be stronger than love. Then he turned his mind towards memories of Stan and knew he was now giving off a very tense feeling that hung over the immediate area in the serene meadow and dampened the mood over the two. The stillness between Joanne and Alex was shared as she too was tense but for different reasons. Although she had greatly enjoyed seeing this place in her personal history and loved showing Alex she knew this could end at any time as she said "I don't understand, they should have come for you by now" as she looked up at the sky and clouds for anything out of the normal.

Neither said a word as they continued to walk in the meadow that was thoroughly consistent in its wide variety of plants and flowers and for the first time Alex began to notice the small insects hopping and flying and felt as though he were a visitor to their world. Every so often Alex would notice Joanne looking to the sky or even behind her and he chose not to ask her what she was searching for, because he knew perfectly well the reason for her investigative stares and glances across the countryside.

Feeling as if he had some history of his own to reveal Alex blurted out "Stan died." Sharing this information made Alex feel vulnerable in numerous ways as Joanne answered, "I thought so. I mean you just kind of gave me that feeling in the tree house, like something had happened but I wasn't going to press you and honestly I was struggling to focus." "I'm surprised they didn't just give you a big file on me and my fucked up life, or do you guys have a paperless office?" said Alex with a strong mixture of anger and sarcasm in his voice as Joanne countered this with "Alex, I was just drawn to you, I wasn't given a lot of information other than what I briefly got to see, trust me." "I'm not mad at you" he said, "Just this situation and how things flew by so fast and how I didn't appreciate it I guess. I regret so much."

Joanne listened as Alex began to speak "Stan and I were tight and because of him and my parents I had a pretty good childhood. Other people bitch about coming from a broken home or what not, but that guy always made the best of it. He was a total history nut but I had the edge on him with math, for some reason I could remember formulas and equations but not who the second man on the moon was." "That was Buzz Aldrin", said Joanne proud of herself for remembering such a trivial piece of information at that very moment.

"Yeah, I should have known that, but anyway we always helped each other out and he was always dragging me places that had something to do with history. Once when we were freshman he dragged me to the museum to see some Viking crap." As this revelation left his mouth Alex became tranquilized in thoughts and memories that coursed through his being and graced him with their own brand of magic and sentiment. But much like a candy that leaves an after taste Alex muttered "And all I did was bitch the whole time instead of enjoy the time with him. I think I wanted to watch a Cubs game or something, Christ I can't remember but it doesn't matter anymore."

"Not true" said Joanne, "Everyone pulls that stunt of 'I'll go but I'll complain' but the that fact that you feel bad means you did learn from it, 'people are people' as that song goes." To counter her logic Alex said "Then why did I let so much just slip by me in my life? I should have learned before all of this." There was no denying the truth behind the words of Alex as they were peppered with regret and remorse. Joanne attempted to stay above the emotional undertow as she asked Alex "So did you work at the museum out of guilt or because you wanted to feel closer to Stan." Alex then smiled and said, "To feel close, always. But what's always bothered me is after we graduated high school I just felt a shift in things." The smile now all but gone from his face Joanne asked, "What do you mean?"

Looking towards the sky with its hypnotic blue seemed to help clear the mind of Alex as he said "He got this idea in high school, I think when we were sophomores to join the ROTC because he really wanted to see the world and by the time we graduated he was all about getting ready for boot camp, mean while I was all about getting my first place and getting laid." An embarrassed and blushing Alex turned to Joanne and offered his apologizes for being so blunt as she simply laughed and said, "That's one of the things an apartment is good for." Returning to the subject at hand Alex added, "Well anyway I was always puzzled as how two guys that were such great friends could lose that. My hair got longer and he got a buzz cut, it was like we could not have ended up more different. Well I did buy some combat boots from an Army Navy store, but he just got his right from the source." This too was a situation that Joanne had gone through much like every other that dared to have a social life and create bonds with another human being as she paused for a moment to think about people she had befriended in her life and how certain unions only lasted a little while and others remained strong until the end and even after.

"So the dog tags were his?" asked Joanne already knowing the answer before he spoke as Alex quietly nodded his head and looked down at his chest and said "Yeah the last time I saw him he called me because he was going to be in town for a day or so on leave before shipping out to some other place and I was such an asshole that I almost lied to get out of meeting him. I just didn't want to feel like a stranger to this person that I once knew." Alex became pensive in his stance while his eyes grew deep in thought as he continued to say "But for some reason I caved and we had dinner and hung out, hit a couple of bars, man we had a great time. We were a little buzzed and he reached into his pocket and pulled out this set of tags and told me the Army fucked up and made him an extra set by mistake and he wanted me to have them."

Joanne listened intently as he went on to describe how they were such a mismatched pair in every bar and club they went to, he the long haired grungy figure accompanied by the clean cut military guy in civilian clothes. "I think that night I realized how much I missed this guy and how much fun he was, I was the one that had changed, I was really jealous of all he had seen and done compared to my misadventures in getting stoned and partying." Alex then took a seat on the ground and once again was back to pressing in small pockets of dirt with his fingers as he said "I promised him I would write and I did but he was killed two months later in some fucking accident, from what I learned from his mom someone hit him with a car while on patrol, it was total fucking bullshit. Just total shit."

Joanne dropped to the soft ground in front of Alex his she detected the clear elevation in anger from him as she reached out and took his hand and said, "Alex our lives are a tapestry of events, experiences, choices, decisions, and emotions. I'll agree you have the right to be upset about Stan, but think for a moment if you had never had that evening with him and never had written him and never had that feeling back. Trust me you'd feel a thousand times worse." Alex quietly shook his head in protest and quietly uttered "I just don't understand" as Joanne countered his reaction with "Here's what you can understand, you were given a choice to hang out with him or let that opportunity slip by and you made the best decision anyone could have made. Your life was better because of that split second decision to say 'yes' and trust me so was his."

Alex wasn't sure if it was the soft and calm touch of her hand or the soothing message in her voice but if her mission was to stifle his mood and make him see the obvious then she succeeded as Alex smiled and said "When he gave me the tags he told me that he was having the best time traveling and wanted me to be connected to it some way. So I put them on and rarely if ever took them off." Alex looked up at Joanne and was hoping to see her smiling but instead wittiness her looking towards the sky with a puzzled expression on her face. "I don't know why you're still with me, I mean that's good, but they are way overdue so we're going to keep moving" she said before asking "Is there anyone you want to see one last time before they arrive?" The weight of the question struck Alex unexpectedly and one person immediately came to mind. "Yeah" he said with a look of steely determination "But I'm not sure how to get there since it's in the present time." "Well we should act while we still can so close your eyes" she said as Alex and Joanne both stood and he took one last look at the meadow as he then felt the warm hands of Joanne clasp over his eyes and oblivion pass through him while in total darkness.

CHAPTER 10

Broadly illustrated abstract styled peacock feathers adorned a large canvas resting on a hefty wooden easel. The original stained legs had long since been covered by beads and drops of falling paint denoting its long and faithful service. Each feather on the canvas had a separate identity yet worked together in the composition with layer upon layer of purples, gold's, and various earth tones to create a peaceful equilibrium. Several feet away a single mug with a faded Van Gogh print sat on the table not far from the still wet paint as warm coffee swirled within the container. The movement of the coffee and the wet paint only served as evidence that the occupant of this small studio was close by and within seconds the crackling sounds of the floor boards signaled her return to the epicenter of creativity.

The room wasn't excessively large nor overly small, but was cramped for space by the bins and containers holding tubes of paint arranged by hue and stored paintbrushes standing bristles up ready to be called into service. Paintings that were complete were displayed on the walls and left little room for the original off white paint of the walls to be seen. Space was further compromised by paintings in various stages of completion that were stacked upon each other with most larger works in the back against the wall as the sizes gradually stepped down towards the middle of the room. The order of the room could be debated on its efficiency and organization, but this workspace belonged to Samantha and it was her corner of the world thus its ergonomics were perfect in her eyes.

Wearing an older faded pair of jeans with the tale tell signs of brush strokes and splattered paint and a black t-shirt that too had seen its fair share of time before a painting in progress. She walked past her latest work on the easel and picked up her mug from the table before sitting on the loan loveseat positioned by the window that overlooked the street below from three stories up. As she pushed her tortoise shell framed glasses up to the bridge of her nose she thought again how it was a below average view as she often was troubled at how the sky could be so blue and to have its harmony disrupted by the jagged skyline. The gray and glass buildings off in the distance, as if mankind were mocking and daring nature with its current and outdated architecture. As if the buildings challenging the sky weren't enough at times she then had to wittiness the pollutions that would often rise from the streets into the air above.

Although she was grateful being able to have windows on one wall that let in a large portion of sunlight she still chose to paint and hang better views of her world on the plain plaster walls in her apartment. With the temperature being warmer than usual Samantha chose to open the only one of two windows that weren't painted shut by either the landlord or the previous tenant and let in the only fresh air the city had to offer. Today was a day when the pollution was not posing a direct threat to the aesthetics of the sky, still a nervous tension was beginning to vibrate through her and to counter its effect she opted to be preemptive with fresh air or warm coffee or resting on her loveseat.

She drummed her fingers on the mug as she took another sip and was torn between devoting her attention towards the outside world or the comfortable confines of her apartment; she even toyed with the thoughts of going for a walk or planning a dinner outing to break the mood that was invading her corner of the world. From her front pocket she quickly retrieved her cell phone and began scanning her address book on the tiny screen as name after name scrolled up and down. The first name she stopped at was David. "Ah David" she said in a low tone knowing she was alone and this fragmented conversation was contained within her studio. As she stared at the name she began to think of many reasons to not make plans with this person. Maybe it was the way he always started each encounter with the best efforts but soon was too consumed in his favorite topic, that being himself.

It was as if every male painter in their mid-forties went through the 'I'm the center of the universe and you should learn from me' phase and felt they had to express to every younger artist that they felt attracted too how they should be together both mentally and physically. Age and experience had given people like David the upper hand in manipulating younger more impressionable artists with his wealth of knowledge and the ability to criticize a piece of work in-depth to the point where it was as if he felt the very things the creator was going through. Perhaps it was experience but she always saw this type of behavior coming a mile away and was guilty of letting him get away with it time after time. However, this evening she was not in the mood for more of his ego driven observations and subversive deception. Samantha knew she would continue this ritual with the next name and the one thereafter. She always had high expectations out of people she would meet and keep in her social circle and often found herself greatly disappointed when they let her down by either deception, shallowness, or simply making the social faux pas that people will make. Samantha even saw the hypocrisy within herself of the high standards she would hold people to this knowing that she was more than likely not able to maintain them either. This internal argument raged on at low volumes until she came to Elise in her address book.

"Yeah Elise" said Samantha in a more upbeat tone sure of her choice now hoping she was available for a few hours as the tremors of uneasiness once again made their presence known. The call was placed and within a second the brassy voice on the other end opened up with a warm greeting "Samantha Honey! Where have you been?" This was why Samantha always liked calling on Elise, her energy and outlook were always positive and contagious as she replied "Hey you, I was just calling to see if you're up for some coffee or something to eat." There wasn't even a pause as Elise immediately answered back "Sure thing girl, give me about twenty minutes and I'll meet you at the Mercury Café, is that cool?" "Yeah, that's great. The Mercury is great," said Samantha before adding "besides I wanted to get your take on the Julia Fish show at the Hoffman gallery." "Yeah, I caught that too but I need to let you go I'm turning a pot and my hands are all clayed up, I'll be there in twenty minutes or so, just need to clean up and head out" said Elise before hanging up the phone, evening without saying goodbye Elise exuded grace which was something Samantha always thought to be in short supply on the locale scene.

Impressing people wasn't on her agenda still Samantha wasn't about to leave her apartment looking a mess so she opted to change into clean pair of jeans and threw on a gray sweater. She also chose a pair of opened toed shoes that showed off her freshly painted toenails done in ruby red that matched her fingernails. After that she took her dark hair down as it fell past her shoulders and bounced to a stop all the while her emotions were spiking with no reason that she could grasp. Still it pushed her to nearly the point of tears as her cat brushed up against her leg in the living room as she grabbed her purse. She reached down and stroked her hand across and through the long apricot colored fur to which he only increased his volume and purred louder by her leg. "Okay baby, I'll be back in a while, just wish me luck with a taxi at this time of day" she said feeling conflicted about leaving her cat wondering if that was the nexus of her emotions, but soon was out of her apartment and making her way to the street outside.

CHAPTER 11

Still in darkness the first sensation that Alex could sense was the smell of acrylic paint, art supplies, and coffee as he soon realized just where he was and was overly excited by his good fortune as he broke free from Joanne's clasped hands. He took several steps away from Joanne knowing full well of his location as he spun around and asked, "How did you know? I mean her, this place?" Crossing her arms and smiling in satisfaction Joanne answered "I had a hunch, but you did this, you led us here" as Alex only halfway paid attention to Joanne as he cut her off by saying "Samantha! Sam! I'm here!" and left the studio to locate the person he so desperately sought out. Joanne didn't have the heart to tell him that communication wasn't possible for him but was unaware of the lesson that he and Nathan had gone over earlier.

From her stationary location Joanne could hear Alex as he furiously searched the small apartment for Samantha and with each room he only exhausted his options until he reappeared before Joanne with a hurt look on his face and asked "Ok, what gives, where is she? I have to see her! Is this some sort of 'moment' that we've arrived at?" His answered was soon revealed in the form of Samantha's blonde cat Darwin, he made a quick lap around the studio and left before Joanne said, "She was supposed to be here, this isn't right. I mean you brought us here because you wanted to locate her." Darwin reappeared then jumped onto the loveseat that Samantha occupied a short time before as the movement of the world outside then caught the attention of Alex as he asked "If this isn't a moment then what's going on?"

As he gazed out the window and look at everyday people milling about he didn't notice Joanne sneak up behind him as she more forcefully clasped her hands over his eyes and held them tightly. This clearly wasn't her nature and held on as Alex struggled and then broke free as he said in an angry tone "Stop with the games already, damn!" as he backed away but had his retreat cut short by a wall as before in Robbie's apartment as Joanne attempted to calm him by saying "Alex I'm not playing games with you, I just need to figure out what happened and why she wasn't here." Knowing his attitude was getting out of hand Alex began feel his options diminish and panic settled in followed by the sting of not seeing Samantha. "I had to stop this, this moment in time. We were live and in the moment when we arrived" said Joanne scanning the face of Alex hoping he was understanding but quickly realizing he wasn't as he answered "This is my 'I don't fucking get it' face" as he pointed towards his chin with his left index finger. His attention broke free from his sarcasm as the scene outside caught his attention. Gone was the kinetic energy of the crowded street, or the people going about their routines and in its place was the still and serene landscape that had now become commonplace to Alex. There were no people to be seen and what cars that could be seen had the visual quality of being parked behind tracing paper.

Joanne's head sank until she was looking at the floor as she said "I broke the rules in bringing you here, I shouldn't have done this but I thought it would help because I could feel how bad you wanted to see her. Even as pissed off as you are right now I can still feel how badly you want her. I could have stopped this action but here we are." Alex listened to all she had to say but responded with a simple "Yeah, well I really wanted to see her" as he nodded his head lightly. The faint image of Darwin remained on the loveseat as Alex had his interest piqued with another part of Joanne's previous statement as he asked "So what rule did you break anyway?" as he waited for her response and continued to stare at the cat in his peaceful state with a look on his face that he somehow sensed the presence of Joanne and Alex.

"Well the rule" said Joanne as she again crossed her arms a little more loosely this time and pursed her lips with her stare returning towards Alex as she added "I took you to this place, a real place in the real world and when I said we were 'live' I meant in the actual moment. Right now you are in Robbie's apartment and he's about to walk out the door and you are about five minutes away from putting the first of two lethal doses of heroin into your body. When I saw Samantha wasn't here I needed to stop this so I put my hands over your eyes. And here we are with the world outside still and proceeding at a crawl." Alex was stupefied by this revelation as he could only answer back "Wow, that's a kicker" as the two of them went silent as each searched for answers or mulled over options quietly until Alex said "Well why don't we just go to Robbie's place. I mean how can my soul be in two places?" With his forehead wrinkled Alex thought he was onto some sort of breakthrough that Joanne surely overlooked until she countered his idea with reality and said, "Because this may sound strange but you have just this one soul, and it's not in your body. Back in the apartment you're on autopilot right now. You're still going to shoot up, and you're going to die. When that happens, and it will, you won't know it because you will be here with me, unless they come for you, then we're both in trouble except I'll get off light."

"So you brought me into the physical world so I could see her?" asked Alex wrestling with his emotions not being able to make heads or tails of anything as Joanne nodded her head in approval. Alex took a seat next to Darwin as he remained perfectly still and he admitted, "I would have really loved to see her just one more time" his voice heavy with regret. "She's talented", said Joanne as she stood before the easel in the center of the room and Alex readily agreed by adding "Yeah she's a lot of great things, she was too good for me anyway" as if resigning himself to defeat as he had done so often in his life. "You think that and in a way you're right, but you're also so wrong" said Joanne not taking her eyes off of the canvas as she then said "Being in my position you are privy to reading emotions both seen and unseen, spoken and unspoken and I know this was more than a brief relationship, that's why you two continued to see each other. It was like you both left something incomplete and you both felt it but never said it." "Yeah you could say that, I never understood why she would call me out of the blue to hang out", said Alex as a smile appeared on his face to which Joanne replied, "Because she was pulling for you and you knew it." The smile all but disappeared from Alex as he felt ashamed for all the times he chose a brief selfish high over an evening with Samantha. But this wasn't always the case as he too made the right choice from time to time to spent extended moments with her instead of feeding his addiction, but these victories were too far and few between to have a lasting impact on his life.

Alex made a move to pet Darwin but stopped short not knowing he was being observed by Joanne, he wanted to caress the cat that was the constant companion of Samantha and much like Reno always looked upon Alex with unconditional love and great acceptance. "Go on and pet him, he'll sense your presence in some small way, I get this feeling that he always liked seeing you" said Joanne as the hand of Alex made contact with his long fur and he remembered just how soft the well-kept cat was. "I swear I can smell her perfume", mumbled Alex as nothing was said in reply from Joanne as her attention was back on the painting in progress.

As Joanne continued to take in the various works of art hanging Alex thought about what had transpired and how in his current state time was of little consequence but yet it was all that mattered and the catch twenty-two was he was beginning to realize it. But like so many things in life it was too late. "So who is David?" asked Joanne breaking the silence as Alex sighed and said, "Just some asshole that she dumped me for, besides how do you know about him?" Joanne continued her lengthy observations of each painting and said, "I don't know, but his name keeps popping up so I needed to ask, it must have been important in all of this. Where do you think women's intuition comes from anyway?"

"Oh gee David, yeah he's some douche bag that she started seeing after me. Some painter that had a good review like four hundred years ago. I don't follow the art scene but in her circles he's one of these pseudo intellects that always wears black and chases younger women. A total bullshit artist, at least that's what I've always thought" he said rolling his eyes as Joanne said "Well I had a feeling this might be a sore spot." His own thoughts then turned to the first time he and David had crossed paths and how Alex was no match for his overwhelming knowledge of art and the world in general. Alex was just beginning to feel at home during a gallery opening and David trumped his mood with his one-upmanship and how he looked at Samantha. The gaze was of that of a collector eyeing his new favored prize like he wasn't viewing Samantha as a person rather something he just had to have all to himself. This was a tactic he had seen other men try and was convinced the opposite sex had their own list of protocol and procedures for derailing a relationship or high jacking a person's heart from another, but this again he also was man enough to know he shared a huge part of the blame.

Joanne once again separated herself and her attention from the paintings and turned towards Alex, the look on her face was one of a person listening perhaps to a faint sound, her eyes remained squinted and she stared off to the left ever so slightly and said "She didn't dump you, she needed to retreat from you. You were just too much for her, the drugs and the emotional toll. Samantha did her best but decided a friendship was a better idea, but not her idea, you really made that decision. She didn't speak with you for a month or so after the split right?" This had the attention of Alex as he began to remember that hard chapter and simply answered "Yeah, it was a tough month." "I get the feeling she was dealing with some heavy stuff she didn't tell you about and watching you go downhill was too much" said Joanne now leaning against the side of the loveseat as she looked out the window as if expecting someone or planning another move to keep them both on the run.

Alex leaned forward without taking his hand off of Darwin; he found the room around him captivating as he said "I always felt right with her, just really safe. When we were too broke to go out we would just stay in as she painted and we listen to music and talked about whatever came to mind. It just seemed so natural to both of us, but in the back of my mind I always knew

I was on borrowed time, my habit would always come back. It was just so strong. I wish others could understand." Joanne looked down for a moment and noticed that he was pushing the sleeve of his plain white shirt up his arm and took note of his surprise of the lack of puncture marks where there once had been many. "Wow" he said, "My arm looks normal for a change and all I had to do was die."

As Joanne put her hand on the shoulder of Alex she seemed to feel every ounce of regret the man could produce as his unspoken honesty was like a full spectrum of color and sound to her as she said "Some people just give others hope and she did that in you. You're not the first person to lose to that drug, and unfortunately you aren't going to be the last. It's just a real son of a bitch, it's evil." As Joanne made this statement both in the room could say nothing as her words began their decrescendo into oblivion and silence settled in. The two began to study the paintings on the walls until Alex quietly muttered "Joanne I know you did your best and I would say take me now and turn me in but if I could stay here until they come for me that would be nice. I know you wanted me to see her just one more time, but to just be here where she once was, and just to share her space. I guess I don't have anything else to add." "I know Alex", said Joanne in calm agreement before saying "I just hope she can survive this."

The two had reached an unspoken agreement to say nothing and just enjoy the silence. Alex paid particular attention to several paintings that he had watched Samantha create and was moved that she still had them rather than to have sold them off. The stillness was broken by three quick knocks on the door of the apartment to which both Alex and Joanne jumped from being startled. Again the knock repeated itself in a quick succession as the hand of Joanne tightened on the shoulder of Alex as if she were holding onto property about to be repossessed. "Um are you expecting someone?" asked Alex not being able to contain or hide his fear to which Joanne replied, "Yes and no, just stay here and let me do the talking" as she stood and let go of Alex with great hesitation and began her short walk across the floor to the door of the studio and around the corner to the living room. The knocking pattern didn't stop its repetition but only became more intense as she got closer to the door. Her hands were shaking from nerves being out of control and she wasn't used to this emotion, at least she couldn't recall feeling this sort of intensity from fear in her current existence. Leaning up against the door Joanne chose not to look through the peephole but instead asked a simple "Hello, who's there?"

From the other side of the door an unmistakable voice

replied, "Joanne, open up it's me Nathan! I'm alone." Joanne pulled open the door and was elated to see her old friend, but as she enthusiastically hugged the unexpected visitor as she asked him "Why did you knock? Why not just come in? I would say you scared us to death, but well you know." With a look and tone of all business Nathan grabbed Joanne by both arms and asked "Joanne, what's going on? Do you know who's looking for you right now?" the look in his eyes said it all and the level of concern was unmistakable. "Yeah I can only imagine", said Joanne "but I did this for a damn good reason, with the way we got sidetracked in the beginning and I just thought I could reach him." This answer was what Nathan had predicted but still found himself angered to hear it admitted as he attempted to put a proper perspective on the events as he said "Hey, he ran. He's the one that screwed up his chance. You were doing your job and he dropped the ball, it's that simple." Joanne broke from his grip and shook her head in opposition, not to the facts but the emotion he was projecting and said "I just felt I needed to give him more time even after time was up. I know that makes absolutely no sense what so ever but I was going with my heart. Come here, we're waiting in his ex-girlfriend's studio" as she motioned Nathan to follow her back to the small room containing the paintings, Alex, and fading hope.

Joanne stuck her head into the room to find a tense

wide eyed Alex still sitting were she had left him. "Hey it's ok, Nathan found us", Joanne said as she then entered the room followed by Nathan in tow as Alex felt a huge sense of relief. Nathan was still puzzled and upset at the entire situation as he walked towards Alex and said "Man I don't even know what to say. It's one thing to endanger yourself but to put others in jeopardy, especially those wanting to help you, now that's low. Just snake in the grass low." Joanne came to the defense of Alex by saying in protest "Nathan that tone isn't helpful right now, this isn't how it was supposed to happen but here we are and I'm just as to blame as he is." She paused as all three fell silent absorbing what was taking place as Nathan felt resentment towards Alex and his seeming total lack of respect towards Joanne or the rules they abide by. Alex felt as though he was caught in a dead end situation ashamed of the life he let slip away and ashamed at how he had failed himself and Joanne in her bid to save him from a fate much worse than he had ever imagined. "I just had this idea that if I could somehow keep on the move, that maybe I, we could turn this around", she said breaking the silence.

"I understand where your feelings are in this", said Nathan crossing his arms "But think about your reputation and about how this will affect your record." Alex watched from the sidelines as Nathan and Joanne engaged in a debate about the rules and what is right and wrong until he could take no more and snapped "Ok, just take me already! Nathan if you feel that strongly then you can take me! Make up some bullshit or something that I ran and Joanne couldn't catch me and I'm just not worth it. Oh wait, that's the truth isn't it? So just take me and get it over with!" This outburst put an end to the back and forth between the two and Nathan turned his attention towards Alex and said, "I can't take you, you're her responsibility and only she can do that." Hearing this Joanne spoke up and said, "That's right and until they pry him away he's mine. There is something to be learned from this and I don't know what it is yet but I'm not letting go, not yet."

Again more silence settled into the room as Joanne added, "Besides aren't we always supposed to be learning from every situation? And you have to admit this definitely a different situation." Nathan took a second to ponder what Joanne had just said and replied, "I know he's going to be your first turn over and the first is never easy." Joanne thought about the truth behind his statement and how she had never turned over anyone for passage to the other side of this after life, the side that nobody wants. She thought about the stories others had shared of their experiences with the standard operating procedure and how they needed to take some time off to recover from the experience. Regaining her focus, she looked at Alex and Nathan and said, "Until they come he's not my first and as far as I'm concerned that's something to work with. Nathan if you are free and feel you want to help it would be appreciated or if you feel you need to back away I understand. It's totally your call."

Nathan's eyes shifted towards the open window as he shook his head back and forth then asked "Why am I'm even listening to you right now?" to which Joanne replied "Because I'm making some sense and you're just too proud to admit it." A brief atmosphere of relief engulfed the room as each began to plan the next move, or at least make the best possible next guess as to what to do. Alex was clueless as to what to suggest so he asked an open ended question to both Nathan and Joanne although aimed more towards Nathan "So how did you find us? I mean this hole in the wall apartment in this city." A slightly more relaxed Nathan said, "Oh Joanne and I have a connection, a bond more like I guess. You know when you know someone so well that you just know their feelings without even asking, or even being there, you just know. Like your best friend" as he took a moment to laugh at how his statement probably came off like a verbal train wreck but it made sense to Alex. He grinned and nodded his head in approval as he looked upon the walls of the apartment and it made even more sense.

Nathan put his hands together producing a loud 'clap' sound and asked "Ok, first things first, why did you come here?" as Nathan looked towards Joanne and she in return glanced towards Alex as he stood from the loveseat and strolled towards the painting on the easel as he struggled with the idea of confessing his feelings about this woman named Samantha. He stared deeply into the mixed hues and the brushwork and said, "I wanted to see her just one more time, she was such a bright spot in my life. I wanted to be everything for her, but I couldn't be. She has this smile, it's the kind you live for if that makes any sense at all?"

"If she's anything likes these paintings then I believe you my friend" said Nathan then adding "Ok, I'll do my best to help you but I can't promise anything and once they show up for you then it's over, got it?" Alex turned and let Nathan know that he understood the conditions of the verbal arrangement as Joanne asked, "Great, now where to? Where might we find her?" to which Alex answered "I don't know but I swear I can feel her, I just don't know where" as all three went into an investigative thought but all knowing that Alex held the answer in the way a compass knows which direction is true north. "Right now Alex you have to think and feel, that's the only way to find this girl, and I mean really feel" said Nathan looking down from the window to the street below as the physical evidence from a moment before began to disappear and fade only to be slowly replaced by the next frame of time as the most obvious object to appear was that of a typical yellow taxi that populated the city from end to end.

The longer Alex sat without desired results the greater his frustration grew inside. He had the feeling of safety from the apartment and loved how Samantha could just make him feel special without trying and always did his best to return the favor but often felt as though he failed her. He began to think about the places the two enjoyed spending time together from bookstores to various coffee shops and pubs, or the independent theatre three blocks away. Alex took his place back on the love seat next to Darwin and sighed as he said "Man this is hard, I just don't know" as he looked up at Nathan and Joanne staring back hoping he had better news from the depths of his mind. Shaking his head he asked Joanne "How did we get here anyway?" as Joanne's face turned to one of concentration, if she was wanting to tell him more than she really knew.

But the truth was she hadn't any more information to help solve the mystery as she answered "We got here together but it was really all you, I just had this feeling of where you wanted to go before you even realized it. But in this case I'm just like a car and you were the driver." She wished this shed more light on the current problem but knew it offered little help as she added, "Although you were really throwing out the feelings for her, that's for sure." Alex smiled in relief and said, "It feels like it did before I started using 'h'. I hate myself for that." Nathan decided to interrupt and said, "It was just too much, that dose you put in your body, I've seen it before." "No I don't mean it like that" said Alex as he corrected himself and added "Well I hate that it killed me, but I hate more that it stole me from her. All the times I would call Robbie or change my plans to take care of it. I should have been stronger. She was worth it, but hey, I guess I was just a user that crossed paths with a cool girl." As this statement left his lips Nathan and Joanne offered up immediate and vocal protests towards the attitude of Alex but, all was lost as he had become fixated on the thesaurus on the top shelf on the other side of studio.

It was her leather bound edition she bought years ago while in college and the gold leaf lettering glowed against the dark leather cover and spine. This book was always a source of fascination with Alex as he had never owned one but always felt language was perhaps his calling. That's what Samantha would tell him due to how often he would open this book while he sat in her studio while she painted and they discussed its contents. Many times she would take note of how his vocabulary was improving in his many attempts to work these newly learned words into his daily conversations, but she could always see how it was his intentions to better himself and impress her. As the verbal onslaught from Joanne and Nathan continued they both noticed that it was having little effect and Alex was officially tuned out as he kept staring that the book on the shelf. Joanne went silent as Nathan continued until Joanne slapped him in the chest to get his attention to which he then took greater notice of fugitivbe and the focus on his face and asked "What is it? What do you see?"

Without speaking Alex raised his hand to point at the book on the shelf as Joanne asked "The thesaurus? What about it?" "That book was always a lot of fun and I know that sounds strange, but I just always loved her thesaurus" said Alex. As Joanne listened to Alex she scanned the shelves for other signs of who this person Samantha is. Perhaps she could help by gaining some sort of insight into her personality by inspecting the items assembled and on display on the bookshelf. From the various sea shells and glass globes used as bookends to the volumes of art books and literature. Samantha clearly had a serious side and obviously loved detective novels. This assessment continued until Joanne's observations were stopped by the thin bright green spine of a book she knew all too well. "The Giving Tree" said Joanne "That's my favorite book. Very to the point and thoughtful, so she must be a rare find to have that on her shelf." Alex began to sense Samantha deep in his chest as he shot to his feet and began shaking his hands uncontrollably as he said "I'm not positive if it's right but I do feel her. It's like she's moving because every time I feel her it just changes." "He could be right," said Nathan "but the million-dollar question is just where?" Alex took several steps towards Joanne and grabbed her hand from her side and raised it to his face as he closed his eyes then covered them with her hand and said, "Let's go, it could be several places but I think I know where."

CHAPTER 12

Samantha stood motionless by the curb not far from the entrance to her building with her hair being tossed to her right with each fresh gust of wind and feeling only slight relief that she was meeting Elise. In most cases an encounter with any friend or attending a social gathering would set her mind in a better direction, especially with Elise because Samantha greatly appreciated everything about her. The honesty and grace with which she could deliver a criticism, or the way she would come to the defense of any friend in need, but Samantha still couldn't calm the swelling waves within her being. With a brief return to reality her arm became out stretched and she made an attempt to hail a cab while in the meantime her mind again wandered on purpose to serve as a distraction from her emotions. For a moment she thought about where she might find new stretcher bars at a better price for a round of commissioned work she had on the horizon, or a better price on gesso, anything to help her margin and not sacrifice quality.

And she thought of her mother and how it had been too long since the two had spoken on the phone or even communicated in any form, not that there were any ill feelings between the two, rather modern life was claiming more of Samantha's time and it was beginning to dawn on her. Then she thought more about what she is to do about David and how he sounded and felt so promising during the inception of their brief relationship and how he turned into a lighter version of disappointment than she was accustomed, to but still disappointing all the same. Knowing we all carry baggage from one relationship to another didn't seem like a plausible excuse for some of his behavior towards her and his judgment of her friends and associates or her life in general. Not that she was hung up on his lesser points and Samantha did realize this man had his better moments and traits, it was just she felt she may have hurried herself towards this person since breaking things off with the conflicted boy known as Alex.

A quick stab of a horn snapped her back into reality as she jolted in surprise as then Samantha heard a voice say "Hey Miss, I don't have all day" as a taxi was now parked in front of her and she felt embarrassment. Samantha had no idea how long she had not been paying attention, "Oh I am so sorry" she said lowering her arm and stepping off the curb and traveling the three feet towards the taxi door. Once inside she again apologized again before saying "1505 West Chicago Avenue please, The Mercury Café" as the yellow car pulled away from the sidewalk and into much lighter traffic than from an hour before.

"Hey not to worry Miss, sorry about frightening you with the horn" said the driver with his thick Hispanic accent now more pronounced in the confines of the taxi "I forget how loud it is outside of the car, you really jumped a mile" he added. Samantha looked up and caught the first name from his driver identification on the dashboard and said, "I'm just being a little spacey today Paul, for some reason I can't seem to focus." She always felt better if she could use the first name of the person she was speaking to even in a situation like this. Samantha found it friendly and respectful and wished more people would follow this practice in their own daily lives. Paul lightly tapped the steering wheel and announced with gusto "Then you Miss have come to the right taxi today, sit back and let me do the focusing! I will take care of you!" This amused Samantha as she smiled and said "Thanks Paul, I knew I could count on you" as she hoped this friendly banter with the unassuming driver would lighten her head and heart as she feared her emotional overtones would be broadcasted to all of those around as she had a tendency to do from time to time, it was a trait that was beyond her control.

The yellow car slinked its way through the maze of city streets lined on either side with older red brick buildings that served as apartments on the upper level and small mom and pop grocery stores and other independently owned businesses on the ground floors. Rusty fire escapes hung from each building as if they were substitute gargoyles but did little to instill fear in the residence that had retreated to the metal structures to enjoy this spring day as it slowly came to a close. This was a part of town that she knew would be going through a transition at some undecided point in the near future, this property was in too good of a location in relationship to the rest of Downtown Chicago. Some would prefer to call it change and some call it progress, but she knew higher rent and condos were coming and Samantha was working hard every day to assure her future in the neighborhood that she both loved and still disapproved of at times. This love hate relationship seemed to be a reoccurring theme in her life and she always put forth her best intentions and efforts all the while always having a backup plan in the works in case things went awry or not according to plan. Maybe it was the idea of just being ready when the change does comes and having options instead of being ushered out of the area against ones financial will, besides the view was always a good excuse to move.

The taxi made a harsh move to the left as Paul took evasive action to avoid an accident causing Samantha to brace herself putting her left hand on the worm out bench seat and the other on the door to her right as Paul said "Crazy people! Everyday more crazy people! Where do they all come from?" Samantha said nothing but felt voyeuristic and invisible to this event that probably plays itself out several times a week or even multiple times a day in the life of Paul the cab driver. "It doesn't do any good to stay angry at them you know," said Paul reminding Samantha that he never once had forgotten the fact that he had a passenger in the backseat. "What do you mean?" she asked having a good idea what he was getting at but choosing to humor him in the conversation or perhaps be surprised as where it might go as he said "Well when I say 'them' I don't mean black, white, yellow, purple, or man or even woman, but people that just don't pay attention. Maybe they're too busy talking on the phone or texting or day dreaming while waiting on a cab."

Samantha came to her own defense and said, "Hey, I'm not crazy, I'm just not focused today, anyway I was called crazy last week, this is supposed to be my sane time now." Changing lanes Paul said with a laugh "Oh I know Miss, I was just seeing if you were paying attention since you claimed to be out of focus, you see, I listen to people." This seemed like a clue to her that he was in tune with her emotional frequency as she took a quieter and guarded approached to her interactions with Paul, if she couldn't figure out what was wrong with her she was not about to have a total stranger analyze the complicated person that she could be at times.

Samantha pulled her phone from her purse to send Elise a text to assure her that she was on the way and would be arriving shortly. With the phone open and the screen glowing she found herself stunned with flashes of panic as she began to slightly tremble on the bench seat. For a moment she wondered if she was paying the price for being a private person and not sharing her deeper emotions with others and opening up. Most people would always second guess Samantha as being very much an extravert due her ability to communicate with most individuals. But she knew this was a skill acquired from years of attending gallery openings and having to rub elbows and jump into impromptu conversations. It was a select group of people that had access to the real Samantha and understood her to be an extremely complex person, and even she didn't quite understand her own wiring. She made an attempt to rally her strength and looked down at the phone then fought to type in "On my way, be there soon" then pressing 'send' she stowed the phone and found herself under more stress than a few moments before.

With her head now leaning against the glass of the rolled up window she watched the road transform from a grainy textured surface with each stop to a smeared gray erasing all of the cracks once the taxi picked up speed. The process repeated itself stop after stop and block after block, but even this did little to calm her as the voice of Paul spoke up and said "Miss, I know it's none of my business, but are you okay? I mean I know I'm just driving a cab, and most people are like 'hey buddy mind your own business' but I feel something is wrong, I always have my 'ear to the street' as I have heard them say." His eyes broke from the rearview mirror as his head swung around to confront Samantha, the car was at a complete stop so she wasn't fearing for her safety and for the first time she was taken by how young the driver was, not the typical older cab driver she was used to dealing with and not appearing a day over twenty-three. His hair was perfectly kept and black as a moonless night with light coffee skin and as he smiled Samantha knew he was a kind soul only showing concern for a complete stranger. As badly as Samantha wanted to open up she simply refused and felt foolish for not evening being able to put her finger on the exact cause of this anxiety, as if she wanted to write a letter but was lacking means of communication. It was then she longed for her thesaurus.

Looking up at Paul she had every intention of lying to him and ushering in another reassurance that she was in good spirits. Her face told a different story as Paul noticed it was not the face of a carefree young woman but was blank and her eyes seemed lost even as she looked forward in a losing argument that she could do little to defend herself in or against. Feeling the taxi lurch forward Samantha noticed the stoplight had changed and the two were in motion once again and she took this opportunity to take stock of herself and regain her composure before any more interrogation began. Without any warning she said "I don't know what's wrong with me. I. I just can't seem to figure myself out today, or last week, or the week before. But today. Today takes the cake."

Paul quickly turned his head towards Samantha and flashed a friendly reassuring smile before returning his eyes to the road ahead as he said, "You know my friend, it's okay to feel lost sometimes because that way you really know when you figure out your direction. Besides everybody has to do it. Just look at me, I drive a cab, so I've had to find my way plenty of times." As Paul continued his sermon on figurative and literal navigation Samantha's mind began to again wander as if he had sparked some sort of reaction in his word usage or even his delivery. From an outer perspective it would appear that the previous conversation was lost on Samantha but deep within her mind the wheels were turning as memory after memory were being stirred up by a combination of Paul's innocent observation and torrents of emotions that would rise and fall.

With her right hand tightly balled into a fist Samantha stared out of the window but nothing of importance was visible and as if everyday life had become a blur. The strangers were all nameless and faceless with just their outlines and clothes giving away their locations and any possible hints to the personalities they might have. Once more she leaned her head against the glass and closed her eyes as the thoughts of life before David entered her mind and she began to suspect that this anxiety was perhaps more of his doing than she had previously thought and her concentration shifted to how things used to be and how this self-doubt that seemed to plaque her today must be his fault. The cab again came to a stop and with her eyes still closed Samantha could distinctly detect the aroma of Chinese food and instead of opening her eyes for a location check she remained still to see where this sensation might take her. "March" she whispered to herself, "Byron Roche Gallery" were the next three words her mouth formed but did not speak as she noticed the world steadily becoming softer and less edgy with each passing second until a steady stream of consciences lead her to March of the previous year and an opening she was attending at the pleading of Elise of all people.

That night Elise had convinced her to meet at a gallery to which Samantha protested greatly before finally caving in and agreeing to go. She had a distinct feeling at the time that she had been a bit of a hermit and Elise made a strong case that Samantha needed to put down her brushes and get out and meet people, especially when inspiration then was lacking and at times almost nonexistent. Her impressions of the gallery were positive as she approached the building that evening under the dark night sky with its bricks painted a soft gray and banners hanging vertically as they swayed in the wind. Puffing out her cheeks and exhaling Samantha said, "Well, here we go" as she dropped her hand onto the metal handle of the glass and aluminum door. A rush of warm air passed her by with the air permeated with the smell of various perfumes and colognes and without even looking beyond the first several people choking the entrance she began to pass judgment on just how the night's events would unfold.

Using her right hand as a wedge and guarding her purse with her left arm she pushed and wove her way up the stairs all the time amazed at how busy this particular opening was and annoyed that it was in fact too busy and the occupancy may act as an obstacle when enjoying the art. Then she noticed all the guys dressed as if they had taken all fashion cues from Details magazine or trying way too hard to emulate the art rock scene from New York of the late 1960's. Samantha had grown tired of both the look and the men that inhabited the clothes and combined with the alcohol she watch being consumed knew this had more of the flavor of a bar or pub than an art gallery. Reaching the top of the stairs the first thing Samantha noticed was yet more people, the men in their skintight black pants or sports coats some wearing narrow neckties made popular in the 1980's. The girls dressed in black, some less and some more on the Goth side. The hypocrisy began to settle in as she realized she too was wearing black pants with a black turtle neck complimented by a red scarf, Samantha felt the only other way to push the art-girl stereo type any further was to wear a beret which she refused to do. Still her determination to find Elise was greater than her sudden shame as she made her way about the room every so often enjoying a song from Bjork that would make its way to the top of the short list of songs being played over a small stereo system in corner.

Hanging against a wall was a large piece that was layer after layer of orange hues. This work caught her attention and she made a short but determined journey across the busy floor for a closer look all the while still clutching her purse and trying to avoid as much physical contact as she could with the other patrons. As it seemed that nobody else was as interested in the exhibit as she was which made for great real estate in front of the large painting as her appreciation for large color fields had deepened over the past several years and this was a good opportunity to take in a new set of works. The temperature in the room was hovering around seventy-eight degrees but she did her best to concentrate on the piece in front of her over the crowd, the music, and the temperature. Dealing with the occasional person bumping into her was acceptable, or even when an inebriated person would stumble by. Samantha was very understanding as long as she was left alone to admire the art, and then came the tap on the shoulder.

Elise wouldn't approach her in such a manner so Samantha ignored the attempt at her attention and continued to look forward. Even the second set of tapping was ignored but the third attempt couldn't be swept under the rug and had to be dealt with. Turning to her left where the source of the intrusion was she saw a man in his early thirties holding a glass of white wine while giving her his best Clark Gable eyes. He was a carbon copy of every other male in the room as he tried to speak above the music and said "Hi, I'm Rick and you are?" there was a pause while Samantha took a moment to size up this pseudo art lover, his hair in short spikes, mirrored sunglasses in the pocket of his brown blazer.

Always up to play 'the game' and to see how far she could test this man's nerves she put on an expression of surprise and delights as she said "Oh hi, I'm totally not interested, I'm here with him" as she pointed at the large orange painting on the wall and swung her attention back towards the direction of work. "Ah, very good" he said brushing off the insult and readying himself for another attempt. "Yeah, that's really good isn't it?" He said waiting for a response that never came as Samantha grew more impatient for Elise to arrive. She could sense him as he moved in closer and could smell the alcohol as he said "I really like the orange, it really glows." This was the breaking point for Samantha as she turned and crossed her arms and gave him a smile sending in a very misguided signal that he was on the right path with her.

"Wow, did you think of that all by yourself? I mean with the way you 'like' the orange?" asked Samantha before stopping short of a full-blown insult. As he began to speak she took pity of him and said "Listen, I'm really here for the art. Not to drink. Not to pick up some guy. I'm sure there are other girls here for that purpose, but not me," as she patted him on the right arm. "Oh!" he said hoping to draw her into a conversation and with a response like that she took the bait and asked "Oh what?" Laughing Rick responded, "I'm sorry. I didn't know you were a lesbian, my bad." "Sorry Rick, I have to ruin that little fantasy for you as well, I'm straight as if that really matters. Just the type of girl that has more class than to pick up some guy at an opening, there's a sports bar down the street." And with that final exchange Samantha feared that she had lost all patience as she worked her way back towards the stairs towards the landing that the bottom of the door. Fishing her phone out of her purse she noticed a missed call form Elise and a voice mail, and never being one to listen to messages Samantha chose to call her fried to inquire on her absence.

Elise picked up on the first ring as Samantha didn't even let her finish her greeting as she said, "Ok, where are you? This is a total meat market, just posers and assholes." "Sam I am so sorry. My car is dead, I left you a message" said Elise as Samantha looked down to avoid further confrontations as a man delivering food opened up the door and began asking the first few people he encountered if they had placed the order. The smell told her it was Asian cuisine and she didn't need to look up to know that so her attention remained focused on the floor and on the phone call. "Honey you have to start checking your voice mail" said Elise, a charge that Samantha was constantly guilty of but never corrected.

Elise spoke up and said in a begging tone "Please don't be mad at me, please." Laughing and showing just a hint of frustration Samantha said, "Some creep just tried to pick me up and then accused me of being a lesbian, if you were here we could have really pissed him off. You always have great one liners. I try but never have the lines you can come up with" she had no sooner said this when she felt the delivery person brush past her. As she spoke with Elise Samantha heard a constantly asked question in a raised voice coming over the crowd and the music playing "Did you order the Chinese food" he asked over and over again. This repeated from person to person and group to group until he was at the top of the stairs and into the main gallery.

"Well why not catch a cab and come over?" ask Elise "I've got a couple of new movies so we can just hang here." Samantha pondered the differences in movies the two enjoyed and although both took great pride in what they chose to view the two were almost polar opposites when it came to their taste in cinema. After a brief void in the conversation Elise injected "Come on, they have something called 'humor' and I'll turn on closed captioning if you want subtitles." Samantha rolled her eyes and said "Ok, but nothing with Mike Myers. Nothing" as she informed Elise she would be getting a cab and heading over as soon as she could. From the top of the stairs again came the voice ringing over the crowd asking, "I'm just looking for the person that ordered this food. Did you order this food?"

Feeling she would have a better view on the street rather than reading the various fliers posted on the bulletin board at the landing of the stairs Samantha pushed the door open and found herself greeted by a rush of cooler air to which she found comforting as she stepped out onto the sidewalk. The sounds of the street replaced the music and crowd hum as she began bobbing her head looking down the avenue for any oncoming taxis. Several more people passed by Samantha and entered the building, and in short order they were met by the man attempting to deliver the Chinese food. He had now worked the entire room and was back to his starting point at the bottom of the stairs with the often repeated question pertaining to the food. Samantha was never one to enjoy a broken record so she decided to place a little distance between herself, the door, and the deliveryman with food. She took an additional ten steps and chose to stare upwards and take in some fresh air before continuing her taxi hunt.

The halo of the city did little to completely block out the stars above as she enjoyed how they shined as a familiar voice began asking a simple question "Excuse me, but did you order this food?" She readied herself to inform this person of his error in thinking she was in the mood for any Asian cuisine this evening, but more importantly to be stern in requesting some privacy on the sidewalk. Quickly turning she drew in a breath and made eye contact with the man holding the small brown paper bag it's bottom slightly darker from moisture as she said "Keep going my friend I'm not the one that ordered the egg rolls" and even as this statement left her lips she felt surprised by the presences of this person. He stood five foot ten inches to her five foot seven inches, his eyes were dark brown with brown hair that fell just into his eyes in the front with an honest smile, not the type of predatory male she had just encountered but rather a genuine guy just trying to do his job. She could tell by the look on his face that her response was a little hurtful after an entire room of people either giving him that same answer or worse. Or even no answer at all and acting as if they were above speaking to a common delivery person.

"Yeah, I had a feeling. You aren't our typical customer. I'm sorry to be a bother" he said as he turned to walk away defeated as Samantha then asked "Hey, what does that mean?" as she was now speaking to the back of his head and could see the light reflecting off of a green windbreaker. The delivery man turned back to face Samantha now feeling like he was in some sort of verbal stand off to which he meant no harm and said "I'm sorry, that just sounded wrong" he stammered as he felt intimidated by her beauty and fought to maintain focus on forming the next sentence and said "It's just. They, you know in there. I guess that's what I'd expect with that behavior, you know, cheap food."

Laughing and finding herself even more curious about this person she asked, "So 'those' people eat cheap food? And what would you mean by 'those' people as she raised one eyebrow waiting for his answer now somewhat enjoying this meeting. "Gee, I don't know. It just didn't feel right in there with all those art types" he said before Samantha quickly cut him off by saying "Ah ha! Now I get it! So by 'those' you mean 'art types' and I just came out of that gallery didn't I? Because you passed me in the landing thus I must be one of 'those art types'" as she concluded with a slight laugh with both eye brows raising and lowering in unison.

With the bag of food swaying quickly and crinkling he raised both hands and said "No no no, I think you have me all wrong. It's just you have a different atmosphere to you, just going out of a limb here since I don't know you from Eve." He looked upwards as he searched for the next constructive set of words and Samantha was all too willing to maintain her silence as she watched patiently. "My gut is telling me you have more class, and by the way I can tell you're not a lesbian. Not that it matters" "Excuse me?" asked Samantha in a sharp manner crossing her arms and taking an offensive stand with only her right leg straight and her left slightly forward and bent at the knee.

"Oh great, I didn't mean it that way, honest!" he said now feeling he had made a fresh enemy as he began to back pedal and looked for an escape before any more damage was done only to realize he had come clean about this observation and said in a clumsy tone "It's just that. When I walked in you caught my attention when you were on the phone, you were talking about some jerk hitting on you or something like that." He had laid the cards on the table and counted the seconds of silence before asking, "So now I'm nosy aren't I?" as he wrinkled his forehead and awaited her answer.

"No. I don't think you're nosy at all, just a victim bad timing and crossing my path," said Samantha unlocking her crossed arms as she clasped her hands behind the small of her back. Both then shared a small collective laugh as she extended her right hand and then said "Hey, let's start over, I'm Samantha, it's nice to meet you." "Hi, I'm Alex" he said as he shook her hand and amazed at how soft and warm her hand was with perfect skin and ruby red nails. "See, I knew you were better than that crowd, now if I could only talk you into buying this food from me. They aren't even answering the number they gave" he said with a wink to which she responded "Now if I did that I'd be your typical customer right?" "Oh no, you're not typical from what I can tell, I just don't want this to go to waste and I can't afford to take a hit on my tips tonight. It's been a slow night and a person stiffing me would just be the tops."

Samantha thought for a second and knew she hated to see food go to waste but wasn't in the mood for egg rolls or wanton soup and also knew her plans later with Elise would include pizza as it was often an unspoken agreement to order one when movies were involved. "Ok, I have a solution" she said holding up an index finger "But you have to go for a stroll so feed your meter." On one hand Alex couldn't believe his luck that he was being invited to accompany Samantha anywhere down the street but was force to make a rather embarrassing confession by saying "Um, I don't have car right now, I road my bike" as he cringed waiting for total social rejection as he kicked himself for simply omitting that piece of information. "Oh" said Samantha "That's really pretty smart living here. I'm on the fence as too get some wheels or not, you own two which is more than I do. Maybe I should start with a unicycle" as she began walking down the street and signaling him to follow.

"So how much?" she asked while looking down an alley that didn't seem very welcoming in the evening light. "Oh for the food" said Alex, "That's going to be $11.43, plus tip" adding a laugh as Samantha reached into her purse and produced twelve dollars while coming to a stop as Alex pocketed the bills. Giving Alex a blank stare Samantha cleared her throat and held up her right hand as Alex, in a clueless fashion asked "What?" before uttering "Oh, change, right" as Samantha said "I'm just fucking with you. Alex you are way way too easy of push over but still fun to make squirm" she said as she took her out stretched fingers and curled them into a small fist and playfully punched his arm. Alex handed the bag and receipt to Samantha as she inserted the crumpled record of the transaction into her purse and began to make her way into the dark alley before Alex abruptly asked "Hey what are you doing?" Setting the bag on a trash can lid Samantha turned towards Alex and said, "I'm not wasting this just letting someone else have it." Turning her attention towards the darkness she said in a louder voice "Fresh free food here! Complements of Samantha and Alex! Hope you like Chinese!"

Samantha emerge from the darkness of the alley with

the light from the street lamps above and the passing traffic sending shadows casting off in various directions behind her and Alex began to wonder just how many dimensions this woman had as if every light source were revealing a different and interesting facet of her personality. "It would be funny if a bunch of homeless 'art-types' came out and grabbed it then you're previous argument would have some merit" said Samantha smiling with the satisfaction that she had done something decent for someone she will never meet. "Why can't you be around all the time when I get stiffed? Then there wouldn't be a problem of people going hungry and I wouldn't have to explain to my boss that I ran into another cheap skate. But then again you may go broke" said Alex trying to keep the conversation alive as Samantha walk past him towards the street and said "I'm made of creativity and style, not money. But I do what I can to help" as Alex could see her search for a taxi had once again started. With her arm extended and feeling like he didn't want the encounter to come to a sudden ending he said "Hey, I know this may sound strange but I could quit my job and we could get coffee or something. Just a thought." Alex continued staring at the back of Samantha and took note of her dark hair and how the curls and waves went past her shoulders and danced in the cool breeze of the spring evening completely covering the red scarf and partial hiding her purse strap.

Samantha turned and flashed a smile as she said, "Now if I did that I would just be contributing to the unemployment problem and the next thing you'll need to do is crash on my couch and that's already claimed by my cat." But in her heart she was strongly considering the offer for coffee and was taken in by his demeanor and seemingly innocent smile. With her attention away from the street and towards Alex she had not noticed the taxi stop on the street in front of her as she quietly studied the impromptu delivery boy she had crossed paths with and how he had an easy going air to him. His voice was calm and his sentence structure showed an awkwardness that in a strange way captivated her immediate attention and left her wanting to ask more questions simply out of curiosity sake.

"I guess I just wouldn't feel right kicking your cat off of the sofa, I just thought I would take a chance and ask but I understand" said Alex shrugging his shoulders with the disappointment of reality peppering his voice as he realized his place was that of a delivery person and a not very successful one at that. With two quick stabs of the horn the taxi shook Samantha with surprise and broke her concentration on Alex as she wondered just how long the cab had been waiting. Not wanting to lose the ride she swung around and quickly put her hand in the door handle and gave it a quick pull to break the seal to the backseat as she looked back at Alex and said

"It looks like fate has spoken in the form of a yellow car, it was nice to meet you Alex maybe some other time" as she completely entered the cab and closed the door. Samantha rattled off the address to Elise's place as the cab driver as he had already begun to pull away from the curb and pick up speed. She turned her head around to search for a glimpse of Alex as his form vanished into the crowd and the night.

But all of this too seemed like so long ago as she opened her eyes Samantha was doubled over with her head almost touching her knees as both hands were now making tight shaking fists pressed against her forehead, her breathing had become so loud and erratic that Paul was forced to pull the car over and said, "Lady, please tell me you're okay I can call for help" as he leaned over the front bench seat. With her head lowered and staring at the dirty floor mat under her shoes Samantha noticed that she had begun to cry and was forcing herself to regain some decorum to reply to Paul before the situation became anymore extraordinary or embarrassing for her or the both of them.

"I'm fine, really I promise," she said raising up in the backseat and wiping her eyes in an attempt to reassure Paul and put down any argument that would suggest otherwise. But to both it was now beyond any doubt that Samantha was wildly stretching the truth and she desperately searched for any exit or even a change of subject but found herself either unwilling or unable to speak with her hand on the door handle ready to escape the confines of the cab.

"We're not far from your stop", said Paul with his voice peaking with optimism "I bet you have some sort of great dinner planned this evening. Yeah I can tell you're going to meet a special person and you will have a good time." Biting her lower lip Samantha could only nod her head in response to Paul as he added "I'm going to put this car in drive and things are going to be better because you are almost there, deal?" Again all Samantha could do is stare out the window and nod as Paul noticed her shallow breathing and only hoped he could deliver her in good time even though they were only blocks away as he put the car back into motion. A buzzing noise had caught the attention of Samantha as she scrambled to find her phone, which had tumbled to the floorboard as she was in a daze earlier. After retrieving the device she noticed a text message from Elise reading:

"I beat you here, I'll order your usual, okay?"

She was still shaking as she responded with a simple:

"k, be there in a min"

Samantha disengaged the phone and inserted it back into her purse and found her wallet as she looked up and saw the concerned eyes of Paul in the rearview mirror and then spied the meter. Paul brought the cab to a halt in front of The Mercury Café as Samantha handed enough to cover the fair and then some as she worked up enough courage to say "Keep the tip." Paul thanked her for the gratuity and once again reassured her that all would be better once from this point on. Samantha wasn't sure if she should or even could believe this stranger but under the circumstances understood that looking for a silver lining was perhaps all she could do as she said, "Thanks Paul, I hope you're right" as she smiled and stepped onto the street and walked towards the café doors.

CHAPTER 13

Samantha found herself walking away from the taxi as it departed and slipped into the stream of anonymous traffic as she had the entrance to The Mercury in her sites. Her view of the two doors was clear and the bright orange painted sign that hung nearly the length of the façade assured Samantha of her location, but with every step she was reminded of her current state as her knees wobbled and began to buckle after every lumbered movement. The enclosed environment of the cab did a sufficient job of muting the outside world but now in this fresh moment as she once again found herself on the sidewalk the sounds of the traffic and pedestrians seemed all but too much for her to absorb. Samantha then put her hands over each ear but even that would do little to silence the overwhelming sounds and her glasses only helped to magnify and assist in the over stimulation as she ruled out a migraine headache.

By crossing this option off of her list only added to the trouble and mystery. Still she fought onward towards the doors of the café that surely must offer some solace from these complicated strains of emotions that could be dealt with easily if presented in single fashion instead they chose to lock arms and take her mind by force and by over whelming numbers.

Being in her current state and without paying a great deal of attention to her actions Samantha found herself within the café with it's perfectly aged hardwood floor and high ceiling covered in tin plates painted white. The clamor of the street was replaced with moody jazz from the 1950's as the aroma of coffee filled the air and the low rumble of conversations between groups as small as two to some gatherings greater than ten in hastily arranged circles or chairs, stools, and tables. Tunnel vision began to cloud her view as she scanned the establishment for Elise among the sea of people mostly decked out in darker clothing in an attempt to match the mood of the place. This establishment was near to her heart as it was a place for artists, poets, and other various creative types that would normally be looked upon as misfits to come together in the heart of the city and be a collective group if only for a little while before retreating to their studios, apartments, or recessed places of comfort.

A cold sweat formed on her skin for a brief moment and she felt lightheaded as she steadied herself on the vacant chair in front of her and closed her eyes to gather her senses before meeting Elise or attempting to venture forward. As always Samantha would do her best to hide her emotions from the public or ignore them like one would an annoying commercial on television. Being in a creative line of work where one deals with emotions on a regular basis was another reason she was a guarded and private person, her inner thoughts and feelings were meant for a canvas not someone's shoulder, but still she had her 'weaker moments' as she called them and let her walls down to a select few, Elise being one of them.

As she opened her eyes the world felt a little more stable as Samantha began to search the room once more with eyes half open and blinking in a more rapid manner then usual as a hand in the distance suddenly shot into the air and began to wave. The coloration of the skin was her first clue due to the skin tone being that of an Asian-American, then tortoise bracelet and silver watch told her it was Elise as the excited hand sliced the air in a frantic effort to signal Samantha. Drawing in a deep breath and stiffening her posture Samantha then extended her arms to her side and balled her hands into fists before stretching the span of each hand wide open to help circulation as she then made the effort to go forward towards Elise and the frantic but friendly hand.

To the average observer the walk across the café would be an easy task to almost anyone, but they were not privy to the tension inside of Samantha as she alone witnessed the room sway and stretch as if in a drug induced state that seemed to intensify the closer she got to Elise who was now standing in anticipation of her arrival. The tight embrace of two arms was the surprising sensation Samantha felt as she realized Elise was hugging her as she couldn't recall the last ten strides towards the table. As if on auto-pilot Samantha returned the hug to her friend as Elise said "Great to see you kiddo! I just got her a little while ago. Some good timing today huh?" "Yeah, yeah definitely" was her simple response as the two broke from each other and Samantha pulled her chair out from the small table for two across from Elise. She could feel the chair jump and bound as if passed over the wood slats that composed the floor and Samantha liked that it wasn't a perfectly flat plain and had character. On the table rested two large ivory colored ceramic mugs as she noticed Elise had ordered her usual white chocolate latte, a drink that had become synonymous with Samantha in any coffee shop the two frequented.

Sitting across from Elise, Samantha liked how her smile

beamed brightly as she said "Hey great choice, we haven't been here in a while" as it was now Samantha's turn to jump headlong into the conversation and said "Uh, yeah I don't think we've been here in a while" as she felt she had her breathing under control with her eyes shifting back and forth as she realized she had in affect repeated Elise nearly verbatim and shook her head in frustration. Not being one to capitalize on too much on an awkward situation Elise laughed and responded with "Must be an echo in here" and reached for her mug. The incandescent lights from above in the chandeliers and other lighting fixtures were one of Samantha's favorite features of the place and normally gave of a soft warm glow to the tables and customers underneath, but were over powered by the amount of daylight coming through the picture windows in the front of the building. This had a positive effect as it reflected off of the straight and shiny black hair of Elise. Samantha had always been secretively jealous of Elise for her beauty and the way she had the Asian-artist mystic going for her, and also for the raw talent she seemed to possess. Not that Samantha was a hack, far from it, but she had the tendency to see the talent in others rather than herself.

Not wasting anytime turning the attention to art Elise said "So, The Hoffman gallery. What did you think of the Julie Fish exhibit?" Without really giving Samantha a chance to reply Elise enthusiastically jumped right back into the conversation in a way Samantha could tell she was excited to talk about it and said "It was cool in a way, like if Andy Warhol were inspired by an old Atari and used the graphics to make floor plans, but that's what I think. The people were pretty cool too for a change, older crowd I guess. But anyway what did you think?" Not that Samantha felt bowled over by her brief monolog or intimidated in anyway, she simply felt tongue tied for the moment and shrugged her shoulders. Embarrassment passed through her as she found the recourses to speak and said apologetically "I'm sorry, that wasn't a real answer, maybe I need this coffee more than I thought." Now Elise felt guilty for pushing the conversation and thought of a better subject to talk about before they warmed up to art.

"So I'm really thinking about getting that cat that was offered to me" said Elise as Samantha fell into focus from a daydream as she added, "Because I've always loved Darwin." She could tell her mind was halfway dialed into the conversation but had missed several moments possibly crucial to the topic at hand. She clung to was the name 'Darwin' to get her back to reality as if that name acted like an anchor. Samantha straightened her back in the chair and said with a smile "Oh one of the kittens from that guy in your building, right?" as Samantha realized she had been avoiding her latte too long and had a sip as Elise said "Yeah all are spoken for except the grey one and I told Mr. Stevens to hold him for me, so he's cool with that. Anyway I want to raise him like you did Darwin, really talk to him all the time to develop his personality. He'll just be my child."

Again the thought of her cat provided an inner comfort to Samantha as she nodded and said "Darwin's always been a total angel." "He's been the best guy in your life", said Elise adding "Plus he's a good man tester." There was truth to this statement as Samantha thought for a moment about how Darwin had always been a very sociable creature and whenever she would begin seeing a different guy the cat would be a good indicator of how long the relationship would last. It was as if he had some sort of special talent at seeing the real person and their motives and whether or not they were truly the type of person that Samantha could spend any length of time with. Her stare remained on the floor as she was lost in thought and for the first time Elise sensed something was amiss with her friend and she decided to let some time pass before interrupting Samantha's peaceful pause.

The hum of the crowd hung over the two and settled down like a heavy fog of sound as Elise noticed the tension around her eyes and how her voice seemed unsteady and lacked the confidence of the Samantha she had known for years. She wanted to steer the conversation back towards the cat and thought about how Darwin had called several people for being of false character and she said "Well Darwin sure pegged David right off of the bat." Once this was said Samantha jumped in her seat like a spring being released and her knee knocked the underside of small table rocking the items sitting on top. Elise was puzzled by this behavior and asked "Hey are you okay? You've hardly touched your coffee and it's like your miles away."

Pressing her hands on the table, her fingers fanned out displaying her red nails as she closed her eyes and said in the calmest voice she could muster "Yes, I'm okay" as she sat still with her eyes closed for some reason not sure if she could open them or if she wanted to. Leaning in closer Elise took stock of her friend and asked, "Do you need a Xanax? It's fine if you do I won't tell anyone." Samantha sat statuesque now squeezing her eyes shut in an attempted to not cry but felt powerless to the mysterious emotions coming to the surface. Now feeling as though things were a bit more serious Elise asked in a stern tone "Is it David? Did he say something to you? You know I'm not the only one that thinks he's the biggest prick ever."

Even with her eyes slammed shut Samantha could hear Elise getting her phone from her purse as she said to

Samantha "I'll call him right now and read him the riot act, it's overdue anyway" as Samantha pulled her eyes open and announced "See I'm fine, no worries" as she reached for the hand of Elise holding the phone and gently closed it in her palm as she added "Fine, see, all good." Again both fell silent with each feeling the other out and seeing who would speak first with Elise staring at Samantha and Samantha looking down on the dark wood table supporting the two mugs. "Okay let's just start over and you can just shake off what's bothering you" said Elise as she raised a mug for a drink not once taking her attention off of Samantha. In turn Samantha reached for her mug in a slow lethargic pace and brought the mug to her mouth as if she were in slow motion. This was no deliberate act because she felt as though she were operating at a mere crawl compared to the rest of the world. Setting her mug on the table Samantha turned her head to the left and looked across the crowd to the large picture window that lined the front of the café. The late afternoon sun was now flooding in as Samantha thought about her loyalties and alliances and how David did test her trust in men and perhaps people in general. But also took comfort in knowing she had an ally such as Elise in confusing times such as these as she felt the next round of panic building within her.

CHAPTER 14

The trio of Alex, Nathan, and Joanne materialized on the sidewalk at another location that Alex felt supreme confidence in which he would find Samantha. "This has to be it" he said, "It just has to be" rubbing his eyes and taking in the still world around him. Nathan grabbed the shoulder of Alex and said, "I don't want to be a wet blanket but this is the seventh place we've been too and we need to make this count" as Alex surveyed the area for any sign of the girl in question. He shook his head in frustration and looked at Joanne and said, "This coin laundry, we've been here a lot" as they all took notice of the room of large industrial washers and dryers on the other side of the dingy unkempt glass. From their vantage point on the sidewalk all could see the typical Laundromat that could be found in most cities with the walls lined with machines on either side. As he found it difficult to make out most of the room due the nonexistent lighting inside Alex pressed his hands and face to the glass to hopefully see more as he said "I don't get it, this place should be really busy, I know I can't see the people but I should be able to see the lights on right?"

Nathan took a few steps back as Joanne advanced a few steps towards Alex and put her hand on his shoulder as he continued his now frantic search from behind the glass. She deeply and quietly sympathized for his dilemma that seemed to worsen with every new option they tried or place he would direct them to as Nathan injected "Damn." This caught the attention of Joanne and Alex as each spun to face Nathan as Alex asked "That's harsh language for someone in your line of work isn't it?" As Nathan put his hands to his side and puffed out his cheeks in apparent exasperation as the defeat that Joanne was feeling began to show on the face of her friend as he said, "That's just honest language. Listen kid, I know this means a lot but we need to maybe plan for things not working out the way you want." "And what does that mean anyway?" asked Alex with an indignant voice "So I should just give up, say 'fuck it' and lay down?" "No! Not in the least" barked Nathan "But let's look at the big picture here, let's think about these places you're taking us to" as Nathan raised his arm and extended his index finger to a point of interest over the shoulder of both Alex and Joanne.

As the two turned to see what Nathan was pointing out she was the first to verbally respond by simply saying, "Damn." Alex walked towards the entrance to the Laundromat and for the first time noticed the white sign with black letters that plainly read 'Closed. Out of Business'. "No. This can't be, I don't understand because I can still feel her, this isn't right" he said putting his hand on the glass as it felt cold and smooth under his fingers and flat palms. In his heart Alex began to realize he was running out of options and felt the hope beginning to recede with the only sure and steady feeling being that of the existence of Samantha. Yet even with this latest round of defeat the feeling grew and was stronger than before.

Breaking the stalemate of silence Joanne said "Why this place Alex, it's not the type of place I see you or her. Tell us about it and maybe that'll help or jog your memory or something." "It's just one of those things that most people go through, laundry day" said Alex as Nathan quietly raised his eyebrows and wrinkled his forehead not expecting that particular answer. As he remained still Alex began to concentrate at deeper levels and said "Samantha and I started doing our laundry together because nobody wants to go the coin laundry alone but taking the bus just seemed like such a drag. So we got her friend Elise involved. She had the car and would provide transportation and in return we would pay for her laundry. It was a nice way to pass a couple of hours that would normally suck and it was a fair trade. I guess it's something only the broke and struggling would understand."

These memories brought a smile to Alex as he looked at Joanne and said, "Yeah, I know it sounds dumb but I always looked forward to laundry day with those two, but really just Samantha." Still in a bit of disbelief Nathan said, "Well, entertainment is where you find it I guess, the only thing I ever enjoyed about Laundromats was leaving. I just can't take the humidity in those places." Alex then readily agreed to this notion as he responded by saying "Tell me about it, we all felt like idiots when we noticed the coffee shop across the street." As if his capacity for speech were suddenly erased from his mind Alex came to a complete verbal halt. With his mouth open slightly and his eyes shifting back and forth he said in a subtle but somewhat audible "Yeah, I think that's it." "What? What's it?" asked Joanne as she had both hands on his arms to which he replied "Across the street. The Mercury."

In unison all three turned their heads towards the large orange sign across the street that clearly spelled out 'The Mercury Café' as Alex then began pulling on

Joanne literally dragging her into the street as he bumped into the ghost like cars feeling frustrated that he couldn't pass through them in his attempt to reach his destination that much faster. The closer he got to the greater the feelings in his chest grew at an almost expediential rate as Alex said "I'm such an idiot, I should have seen this earlier" "Better late than never" responded Joanne as the two grazed the edge of a car forming in front of them. The details of the place began flooding his senses as he matched them up against his memory as if he needed some sort of verification that this was real and not some sort of cruel hoax being perpetrated against him. But Alex had no reason to find Joanne untrustworthy in anyway as she had proven herself to be one with his happiness in mind. He could also find nothing out of place and was convinced that this indeed was the place he was seeking

Reaching the front door Alex had a world of momentum with him as he suddenly felt a pulling sensation fighting him but this only made him work that much harder to pull the double doors open and enter. "Alex, wait!" said Joanne in an attempt to pull him to a stop, "Not yet, I need to explain a few things first" as they both struggled with Alex winning this contest. "No time, I have to get in there" was all he managed to get out before being knocked to the ground like a dead weight, there was no mistake that Nathan had put an end to his forward march. "When Joanne says stop then you stop, got it?" said Nathan holding Alex to the ground. "Nathan, really?" asked Joanne a little upset by his actions as Nathan calmly turned towards Joanne and said "I told this boy not to step out of line with you." Knowing this was part of their earlier agreement Alex said in a defeated tone "He's right, we agreed to this. Can I get up now?" "Sure" said Nathan "Now that we again have a clear understanding" as an embarrassed Alex was pulled up by Nathan. "Go on, I'm all ears" said Alex as he wanted nothing more in the world to see Samantha one last time.

"Good" said Joanne still a little upset with Nathan's heavy handed but effective tactics "Earlier in her apartment I told you we were a little behind the time when you died" Alex said nothing but nodded his head to assure her he understood but wanted to proceed onward. Joanne looked at Nathan and then back towards Alex and continued by saying, "We're going to go in there and when that happens it'll be just like before in her apartment. Time will pick up and continue and time becomes very very limited, is that clear?" "It's clear I get it" said Alex "Let's go already" as she covered his eyes and Nathan reached for the door and handle and pushed it open as the three crossed the threshold into the café and Alex was immediately bombarded with the smell of coffee and the sound of jazz music, but most of all the feeling in his chest was now to the point where he thought it might explode. He didn't need any more of a hint to tell him he had arrived as he reached up and pulled her hands away from his face. The three carefully looked over the crowd with only one really knowing the description of the person they sought.

"There!" said Alex excited by the vision of the back of her long dark curly hair and seeing the face of Elise only helped guarantee his confirmation as he and Joanne hurried through the crowd avoiding people and tables as they seemed to form some sort of partially moving maze and obstacle course until Alex stood just two feet away from Samantha and became motionless as he was in awe of her presence. His observations continued quietly as he worked a circular pattern around the small table where Samantha and Elise sat and listen to the conversation as it proceeded. "She is really pretty", said Joanne from the sidelines as she was now joined with Nathan by her side as he added his opinion by saying "So that's the legendary and highly sought after Samantha. Well well well Alex you weren't kidding where you. She's hot." Alex looked up with a smile and said, "You've got that right and her personality is even better" as the smile ran away from his face he added "Man did I screw everything up." Without breaking his attention from Samantha he heard Joanne say, "Don't act like that now, we aren't here so you can be that way" as Alex now began to notice problems and errors with this scene.

From his vantage point it looked as if Samantha had a heavy heart due to the lack of any smile that he was used to seeing, Alex could feel the tension around Samantha as she spoke to Elise and said "Fine, see, all good" but both Elise and the invisible Alex knew her better than that and also knew she could be a tough case to solve when it came to getting her to confess what was on her mind. This was when Alex looked up at Joanne with a look of distress as Elise said, "Okay let's just start over and you can just shake off what's bothering you." Alex then noticed her hands were trembling as she attempted to hold the coffee mug and had to set it back down on the table as to not spill its contents after taking a sip. "What's wrong here?" asked Alex of Joanne, "This isn't right, she's not acting right!" "I don't know" stammered Joanne, "You know her better than we do." But Joanne didn't need Alex to tell her that this wasn't going smooth as she turned towards Nathan for any ideas. He was already formulating thoughts about what might be happening.

Once she set the mug back on the table Samantha threw her head back and sucked in a deep breath in a sudden unexpected action that startled both Alex and Elise. She then covered her eyes with both hands and went still until small spasms shook her chest and the sound of crying could be heard from under her palms.

"Samantha honey, please tell me what's wrong, please"
asked Elise as Alex, Joanne, and Nathan waited by the
table for her response until she wiped the away the
beginnings of her tears and said in timid voice "I really
don't know." Then backed up by a confused looked as
Elise searched her purse for a Kleenex and handed
several to Samantha which now had pink in her eyes
where they were once white. After taking a few breaths
Samantha said, "You know maybe it's a panic attack or
something like that. I'll be fine after I just calm down."
"Don't make me slip this Xanax into your coffee because
I'll do it!" joked Elise in an attempt to lighten the mood
as the concern from Alex became greater and he asked
Joanne "Can you help her? Please?" as his attention was
now fully focused on Samantha and her swaying
emotions.

Nathan pulled Joanne aside and asked "Any ideas on
this one? Maybe we should get him out of here because
this isn't going down like you two had planned." Joanne
rubbed her forehead in thought as she tried to once
again fall back on her training before quickly coming to
the conclusion that her training never covered breaking
the rules as several feet away she heard Samantha burst
into tears and Alex exclaim "Please do something!"
"Man just calm down" shouted Nathan "We're working
on it" as Alex continued his circling of the table. Off in
the distance the wall clock caught Joanne's attention
and she said to Nathan "I think I know what's going on

here and if I'm right this is going to go bad." The crying continued as Alex began pleading with Samantha "Please don't baby, I'm right here I'm safe" and Elise was now leaning across the table to comfort her in vain. "What's going on?" asked Nathan clueless as to what explanation Joanne might give.

"Samantha just knows something is up, she knows something's not right. Maybe it's us just being here. When I got to him it was 5:54. He passed at 5:55" as Nathan now took notice of the clock and said "Yeah, I think you may be right" as the large hand passed the hash mark on the face of the older clock clearly showing the time as 5:53 and counting. "Should we get him out of here?" asked Nathan as Joanne shook her head in confusion and said, "I just don't know, but this can't go on like this." Samantha now had her head on the tabletop and was crying in a volume that most people around could hear and Alex for the first time placed his hand on her head and said in a loud voice "Joanne, Nathan, please!"

Nathan now decided that he should take a little more command of the problem and said "Alex, we need to go now. I'm sorry this didn't work out but we can't be here anymore" his voice reminding Joanne and Alex of his past vocation in law enforcement. He took several steps towards Alex and forcefully grabbed his arm and pulled. This reaction only made Alex want to fight and stay but to no avail as all he could do under the sudden duress was brush his hand past Samantha's hair which made a small section shift as though moved by the wind. After this brief encounter Samantha began crying even louder now attracting a small crowd of onlookers. Elise had made the decision to get her out the café and said, "Come on honey you need to leave" as she reached and grabbed her hand and led her away from the table.

Alex was beyond controllable as he fought to break free from the overpowering Nathan while screaming, "Let go you fucker! Let me go!" so loud that he was sure the living could hear his frantic plea. Joanne pushed open the doors to the café as the living assumed it was a strong wind and all three found themselves outside as the sound of everyday life replaced the serene feel of the coffee shop. Joanne felt a crushing guilt that made it difficult for her to express her thoughts. The three managed to get about fifteen feet from the door as Nathan clearly had control of Alex and asked of Joanne "So now what?" in a tone that could have sounded sarcastic if she hadn't known Nathan any better than she did. She had little time to put a chain of thoughts together as Elise and Samantha emerged from the café, Elise was assisting Samantha with walking as she was clearly shaken by something she didn't quite understand. The time struck 5:55 and Samantha cried and then buckled under her own weight until she was on her knees and crying. Several strangers offered their assistants to Elise as she gladly accepted and the two kindly men helped Samantha up as the small group walked towards the car Elise normally drove.

"Alex" said Joanna "I'm so so sorry it happened like this, I wanted it to be different." Alex and Nathan had finally given up their duel for control as Alex too fell to the pavement a broken man with all hope seemingly gone. His head fell forward and his eyes were closed as he said "So that's it. I guess it's over. My whole life was a total waste, I left nothing behind, I made no impression. Nothing." Nathan leaned up against the glass window and looked at Joanne for answers but also in a gaze that showed he thoroughly understood her actions and motivations. Alex broke the silence of the three and asked "So do we wait here for them to come for me or should be go back to my body and run the clock out at Robbie's?" Looking forward Alex noticed the large hand of Nathan being offered to him in a gesture to rise up as he slowly watched the dark hair of Samantha disappear into the purple subcompact owned by Elise. "There she goes" was all Alex could manage to say.

"You know you're wrong", said Nathan as this caught the attention of Joanne and Alex as he asked "In what way?"

"Your life was not a total waste, you made an impression on her."

"How? Because I don't see that it did a whole lot of good"

Seeing the conversation unfold between the two seemed to give Joanne the strength she needed as she spoke up "Samantha was having a melt down because she knew something was very wrong but more importantly it involved you. At first I thought it might be because of our presence, but then I noticed the time. It's now 5:57 and you've been dead about two minutes and I think she somehow sensed it, that's the only explanation I can offer up. You two had a bond that really meant a lot to her, a lot more than you knew."

"But it doesn't do anyone any good now, just take me back to where ever it is to finish this out" said Alex his attention locked in the direction of where he had last seen Samantha as all Joanne could say in a sullen tone was "This is going to devastate her." This bleak prediction startled Alex as he swung his head back

towards Joanne and asked, "What do you mean?"
Joanne didn't want to be the barer of such news at this
hour but felt total honesty was needed as she said, "It
was like when you lost Stan, but I have a feeling this'll
be much worse." "So I get to upset and disappoint
people even in death, wow that's just great" said Alex
shaking his head before signaling the other two "We'll
let's get this over with." Closing his eyes he pointed to
them and said, "Come on, let's get back to the scene of
the crime and do this." Joanne sighed disappointed as
she covered his eyes and looked at Nathan as she too
had lost this struggle and knew the only thing left to do
was return to the apartment of Robbie where the
lifeless body of Alex lay.

CHAPTER 15

Doubled over in the front seat Samantha wept while looking at the floorboard of the car and thought of how just a short time before she was in this same position while in the taxi as Elise did her best to comfort her friend but had little success in the matter. It was as if someone had released the tourniquet restraining her emotions as she found herself too overwhelmed to speak or answer the most basic question put forth by Elise. "Sam hunny, you're scaring me. How can I help?" Elise asked as she drove while concentrating half of her attention on the road and the other half on Samantha. Like the taxi ride earlier she could feel the world pass by but lacked the strength to respond in any manner. After locating some courage, she pulled herself up and sat back in the seat of the car as Elise looked over at her friend. Her eyes were now red with smeared make-up and a runny nose. Samantha's hair was the only part or her being that seemed to stay in place as it naturally fell back onto her shoulders and beyond.

"Do I need to pull the car over hunny?" asked Elise "Is there any place you need to go?" The lack of a response from Samantha only helped to frighten Elise as her friend then tensed up and fell towards the passenger window as Elise said "Anywhere you want to go you just let me know. Do you want to go home, I bet Darwin misses you." Again nothing but the continued crying of Samantha filled the car as Elise struggled over what to do next or how to help her friend. As long as the two had known each other Elise had never seen such behavior from Samantha, even in the most stressful of times she managed to pull things together and rise above any problems or obstacles. "I don't know", said Samantha in a voice that barely registered as audible as Elise quickly asked "What is it, what don't you know?"

"Why do I feel like this? It just hurts."

"Your head? Your stomach? Your back? What hurts?"

"It - It's hard to explain"

"Just take your time I'm here"

The comforting words of Elise did little to combat the torment as Samantha lunged forward and forcefully put her head on the dashboard and increased the intensity of her crying as she began rifling through her purse searching for her migraine medicine as she had past the point of desperation and begged for mercy. She accidentally unhooked the clasp on her wallet and its contents spilled and became mixed with various items like her cell phone and makeup. Her tears made it difficult to see as she felt Elise place her hand on her back and Samantha did her best to recover the cards and papers from the bottom of her purse. Her hand found a familiar texture as she wiped her eyes and looked down onto a receipt from a Chinese takeout restaurant.

The object of wrinkled and faded paper distracted her so much so that she ceased crying and could only concentrate on how this little piece of paper played a key role in her life and why she still carried the item. It was calming and almost hypnotic as she thought back to what seemed like not so long ago. Before the confusion of job changes and money or the modern problems that had slowly but surely crept in and made life the complicated spectacle that she had often read about, but somehow managed to keep at bay. And this little piece of paper then forced a much need break and she thought back to a less troublesome time.

Samantha's mind began to wander to a fond memory buried only where she knew where to find it. That day, after a brief rain the city seemed to be coated in a light gloss provided by the grey clouds above that seemed to give the lights, buildings, cars, and people a hazy reflection on the pavement. Too on this day Samantha felt foolish and a little bit awkward as she stood in her beige raincoat forty feet and on the other side of the street from the small Chinese takeout place as she held the crumpled receipt in her hand that had the previous Friday evenings date stamped in the bluish purple ink common with most cash registers. Feeling as though she were a cop on a stake-out Samantha made several attempts to talk herself out of this act before it spiraled into areas of embarrassment or shame.

There was contemplation and stalling as she put this thought against the larger argument of what had been on her mind the past seven days. She wanted to fight the urge to move closer to the large neon sign that hung in the window and glowed bright red against the florescent lights within. Samantha compared the name on the receipt with the name glowing in the window, which erased any doubt that she had about her location. Noticing a few customers and several men toiling behind a counter with the occasional rise of steam from the narrow kitchen that was busy behind the cash register. She kept time by checking her watch every few minutes and had to wonder if she had been noticed by the lone man that seemed to be responsible for calling back the orders and ringing up the customers. Although she couldn't hear his voice she could tell by his actions that he was clearly in charge.

"What the hell?" she asked of herself as time began to tick away and soon went from a few minutes to twenty since she had first arrived and started keeping track of this endeavor. "Why?" she then asked quietly, "Why oh why am I even doing this? A girl should not have to do this." Her powers of observation were strong and after a while she had a good idea of the working relationship and duties of those who occupied a place behind the counter. Besides the man at the cash register in his bright red t-shirt the other men wore paper hats or hair nets and white t-shirts that were off color from sweat and food stains, like they wore the calling card of their hard work and vocation in their chests and sleeves. This distraction would only last for so long and she knew soon it would be time for action but in the meantime decided that a call to a more level headed individual was needed to break this impasse.

Her phone was soon out and on with her fingers dialing a number that she knew by heart and was optimistic about its prospects until the third ring. Soon the fourth ring had come and gone and the call had gone to voicemail and with it any hope she could turn to another diversion from this view across the street. A familiar voice announced the greeting as it said "Hi you've called my phone but I'm not available, just leave a message." "Hi mom, it's me", said Samantha "I just wanted to give you a quick call and say hello. You should change your message and punch it up a little bit. Yeah it needs some pizzazz in a big way." Her focused was once again trained on the red sign as she felt the inevitable draw to the neon as she decided to finish her call by saying "Well, just call me when you're free. Bye." She then slipped her phone back into her purse and then watched the orange hand in the crosswalk sign fade into a symbol of a person walking and thought to herself "Well if that's not an obvious hint" as she stepped into the street and began her small journey.

Pushing on the door she was greeted by the chime of bells suspended above and then by the overpowering smell of Chinese food, particularly soy sauce. The room was decked out in shiny linoleum, which only helped to reflect the bright white light to a greater intensity. "Yes, can I help you?" asked the stout Asian man behind the counter wearing the red shirt "Do you have an order to pick-up?" "No, no I don't" she said in reply stepping closer to the counter until she was now at the chest high half-wall. As the phone rang he grabbed a menu and slid it across the counter top and said, "Here, look at the menu. I'll be with you in a second" then picked up the receiver and gave the greeting he must give a thousand times a week or more. Using the menu to further distract herself from the mission at hand she glanced at it over and over hoping to stir her appetite but to no avail. All the words seemed to run together and the type made little to no sense as more time passed and the focus and determination she once had was now being lost to fear and second guessing. "Thanks but I've changed my mind" said Samantha as she slid to menu back to the man behind the counter who simply waved and didn't take his attention off of the phone call as she made a hasty retreat to the door as the bells announced her exit back into the soggy world.

Her time in the small restaurant was brief but was long enough to make her appreciate the smell of rain all over again, even in this urban setting. Shaking her head Samantha proceeded west as she mumbled in a low tone "Okay, that was almost embarrassing." Approximately fifteen steps after leaving the establishment she heard in voice in the distance "Hey! Hey you! In the coat!" Although there were many others on the sidewalk and most were wearing outerwear of various descriptions she had a feeling of certainty that this plea was meant for her. It was the tone of the voice that stopped her in her tracks as she quickly turned to see Alex dismounting his bike in front of the restaurant and setting it aside without even locking it for safe keeping. Wearing the same green jacket from the previous encounter he was thoroughly soaked from head to toe as he ran closer to her.

"Oh my God, Samantha right?" he said excitedly "I can't believe I crossed paths with you, wow!" as she concealed the receipt in her hand and brushed her hair to the side with her other free hand. "Yeah what a strange thing to have happened" she said with a smile "It's Alex if I remember correctly" playing her part as calm, cool, and collected. "You remembered", he said twisting his head slightly returning the smile.

"Yes I did."

"So what brings you to this part of town anyway, another opening or something like that? Or are you solving a mystery in that coat?"

"I had to drop of a commission piece and was just going for a walk, I love the rain."

"Me too, expect when working, then it can suck" said Alex pointing to the matted down and wet hair wet as stray drops traced their way down his face and failed to notice the lack of an umbrella on Samantha's person as he then added "But it's a hazard of the job, I hope your painting didn't get wet." She had hoped he wasn't seeing right through her story and knew there were few in this neighborhood that would be purchasing a commissioned art piece as she quickly responded by saying "Nope, just wrapped it well, safe and sound, can never be too safe." "That's good" said Alex as his mind raced looking for something to say to hold the attention of Samantha just a few seconds longer as she put both hands in her pocket almost sensing his precarious situation until he finally said "While you're here I just wanted to say I'm sorry about asking you out for coffee last week, I mean in that way, it wasn't cool." "In what way?" she asked squinting her left eye curious as to what his explanation would be but not wanting to tell him he did nothing wrong.

"I just came off like a weirdo or something asking you to get coffee and then saying I'd quit my job on top of it, not my finest moment" said Alex laying his apology at the feet of Samantha as she took her left hand from her pocket being sure to leave the receipt behind as she playfully punched his arm through the rain saturated sleeve. "Don't beat yourself up Alex, a guy willing to quit his job for a girl is a big deal, but a guy with a job is where it's at" she said hoping he was getting the signal she was trying to send with her eyes "We tend to like that in guys. You know, the whole employment thing."

Alex nodded his head and felt he was standing on the edge of a larger moment and knew if he didn't take just one more chance he would forever be upset with himself and said with a coy smile "Well, how about this suggestion" as he paused and Samantha playfully leaned forward brushing the hair back from her left ear exposing several small piercing that caught his attention and nearly derailed his thoughts. As he regained his ability to express himself he said "What if I finished my shift" adding another pause as Samantha raised both eyebrows "And get cleaned up and we have coffee later this evening? That is if you're free." As he finished his request for her company he shrugged both shoulders and gave her a look that was boarder line comedy and boarder line evening news. As if she wanted to draw this torment out a little longer Samantha gave a long pause before relaxing her leaning stance and said "Sure, what time?" The eyes of Alex became wide and alive as he began to doubt his perception of the past several moments and stammered to say "Oh. Um I get off work at 9:30, is that too late?" "No that's fine", said Samantha taking note of the surprise on his face but saying nothing in reaction.

"Alex! Get in here!" said the voice from down the street as Samantha leaned over to look past him and saw the man in the red shift with his head sticking out of the door "I have food to go out!" "Oh crap, I have to go" he said not wanting this particular moment to ever end but knowing he had to let go as Alex added "We'll talk when I get off and then have a nice cup of coffee" as he began to turn and the man disappeared back into the restaurant. "Just a second" said Samantha stopping Alex, "I need your number and you need mine, that's how making plans works" as she laughed. As he gave her his number she entered it into her phone and called him so he would have her information and said "Okay then, you do you're thing and call me when you leave, we'll just wing it from there." "You got it, I'll call you" said a stunned Alex as he turned towards the little hole in the wall restaurant and knew his remaining hours on the clock would seem like an eternity.

But now in the car this encounter seemed forever ago and with her head against the glove compartment Samantha remained as still as she could while the occasional emotional charge would course through her body and made her cry and shake as the receipt danced about in her field of vision with each bump the car encountered. She wasn't sure how long she had been distracted with this memory but it filled her with a serene peace that was something she hadn't encountered in so long. "Samantha, do you know where you want to go?" asked Elise as she could feel each staggered breath that Samantha produced. The question was simple, as simple as the emotions that now seemed too obvious as all Samantha could do was say "Alex." Increased levels of panic now shot through Samantha as she sat up in the seat so quickly she pinned the hand of Elise back and drew in a rapid and long breath. With the receipt clutched in her hand Samantha was as stiff as a board with her other hand covering her mouth to frightened to say the name that seemed to be the focus of this strife.

"What?" asked Elise "Hunny what about Alex? I don't understand" as she pulled the car into a local grocery store parking lot and took stock of Samantha. The look on her face was one of a person that had seen a ghost as her hand remained locked over her mouth muffling her crying as she tried to speak and say "Alex" only to have it muted by fear as more crying ensued. Quickly securing the car in 'park' Elise turned to the now frantic and nearly out of control Samantha and put both hands on her shoulder "You need to talk to me or I can't help you!" said Elise looking her right in the eyes.

"Something!" said Samantha in between sharp breaths "Something's wrong! Really wrong!"

"What, who? Is it Alex?"

"Yes!"

"How do you know, did he call you?"

"No!"

"Sweetie this is crazy, you need to calm down"

"No! - Oh no! I'm right I know it!"

For the first time Elise noticed the small piece of paper clutched tightly in the grip in the hand of Samantha and inquired about its purpose as she asked "What's the receipt from?" "This is from where he used to work, he gave it to me the night we met" said Samantha looking back at Elise who wore a puzzled expression. "This receipt is how I found him, when I saw it in my purse it just made sense to me" she said gasping for each breath. Samantha stared at Elise with wide eyes and frozen still in the seat waiting for her to make the next move as both were overtaken and confused by the events of the past 20 minutes since they left The Mercury Café. Wanting to take more control of the situation Elise spoke up as she held Samantha and said "Listen hunny, you need to call him. He'll tell you everything is fine. Is that okay, will that work?" Kicking herself for not seeing the obvious Samantha rapidly nodded her head as she rubbed the tears from her eyes and retrieved her phone. "Go one and call him, you'll see everything is fine" said Elise as Samantha dialed his number and nervously pressed the 'send' button.

CHAPTER 16

The ambulance and police car from earlier were still in place however now they stood even more pronounced parked on the street in front of the courtyard to Robbie's apartment. The lines and curves of the vehicle structures were almost completely formed and gone was the guessing that might take place while watching these objects form, their identity was clear and could not be mistaken. "Well this is it", said Nathan pointing out what all knew to be obvious as all three then took a moment to stare at each other in repose and thought. The square and almost unflinching chin of Nathan, a characteristic that he gained through years of work as a police officer and seeing the worst that people could be had hardened him and in a way he used as a defense. So strong was this that he carried it with him into his current existence and knew it was his issue to overcome. The defeated eyes of Joanne that always had the best intentions for those around her and could fail to see the shortcomings in her plans. Her motto in life was to never give up and she still clung to this belief even now as she now stood in the shadow of its flawed ideal. She began to realize where she may have failed Alex but was left speechless in the aftermath. Earlier in the few moments when Alex came back with Nathan her attitude was in maladjustment and perhaps this was why this mission had failed.

Alex stood in place with only his head swiveling and changing directions to take in any final memories of this place as well as Samantha, that is if he were allowed to take such thoughts with him where he was going. The idea of being denied memories of Samantha was to him the greatest form of hell. He thought about what he would miss the most and what he will never get to accomplish and how these plans which were put off for so long will remain an unfinished work much like his life. But mostly his thoughts and feelings were with and about Samantha. Remembering how both would pass the time in her apartment like a couple would, with meager means knowing entertainment is where you find it. Or being dragged almost kicking to the art museum to see something he had no knowledge of, but began an interest for because she loved it so much. Or the way she stared so intently at a painting in progress as though the next brush stroke were going to make or break the piece and how much he loved the look on her face. He was also remembering the tone of her voice and how even in the worst of moods she had a characteristic that he loved to be around. And lastly he wanted to hang on to the sound of her laughter that always rang in his ear like a sweet bell.

In his hand he felt something warm and soft and looked down to realize that Joanne was holding it in comfort as she said, "Alex I'm so very sorry. This isn't how I wanted this to be, I really did have the best intentions." Alex gripped her hand lightly and said in response "I know you didn't want it this way, I just messed up. You could have been doing your thing to help me but I bolted, I know this is on me." Nathan kept his silence because he knew he had a habit of saying the wrong things that usually involved his opinion. "I should have been bigger than my feelings of disappointment towards you. It was like I lost all sense of who I am, that's not how I operate and I couldn't have picked a worse time to act like that" she said adding "And I hate that we're at the end of the line."

Nathan spoke up and said "I have to give it to you young man, while looking for Samantha you were putting up quite a fight. I love that kind of determination in people.

And when you found her, I saw that fire in you." "But it wasn't enough" said Alex putting an end to the slight smile on the face of Nathan then saying "I just wish I could have communicated with her, just to tell her that I loved her just once more, just something." "I understand", replied Joanne "Believe me I understand."

"Sometimes I hate this system we have!" said an enraged Nathan in an outburst that neither Alex nor Joanne expected "Just fucking hate it!" as his hands flew into the air in a rage. "Nathan this isn't the time for that" she said wanting to put a cap on his emotions as he replied "Sometimes when you're a cop you see things that you wish you didn't have to do, but you have to follow the law. Even if it seems nuts, you do it because you put on that badge." Now Joanne had resorted to giving Nathan a stern look in hopes of softening his edge at this moment as Nathan said "Sure this guy screwed up in his life and then this, but look at him, I think he's learned something and it's too late and now 'we' can't do a damn thing about it." Letting go of Alex's hand, Joanne marched over to where Nathan was standing and grabbed his arm to lead him a distance a little further away as she said "Just what do you think you're doing? We need to be calm with him. I don't know when they are going to be here be we need to look like we're under control." Alex could only see the flailing of arms and exchange of emotions in a whispered tone as to where he couldn't hear the entire conversation.

"Why now Nathan, why the vested interest in this guy? Because you sure didn't show it earlier" she said as he replied, "Because he showed me he's a fighter. You can hear it in his voice, the regret. And we're going to have to get over letting him go. Man this just sucks! And I'm sorry but I can't hold my tongue anymore and I know you feel the same." Joanne nodded her head and looked at Nathan and then posed a simple question "So what would you do if that were you?" Sticking out his chest Nathan proudly said "I'll tell you what I'd do given the choice is I'd climb back into my body and fight. I'd kick, punch, bite, and claw my way back to reality, that's what I'd do." "So why can't I?" asked Alex as Joanne and Nathan had not noticed him walk up to the both of them as they had their spirited debate. Having caught the two off guard Joanne was the first to speak and said, "Because it's against the rules, when you're out of your body then you're supposed to stay out and that's it."

The answer Joanne provided did little to satisfy Alex as he immediately began a simple but strong protest by saying "You did it." She knew exactly what point he was trying to make and did not want to provide any false hope at a time like this. Before she could answer to this

Nathan spoke up and asked "You mean you told him you got back into your body once?" "Well, I did it twice really, I told Alex how I got out when I was in the hospital and Jacob was there. But I also did it years earlier in a similar situation." "Wow" was all Nathan could say to this revelation before Alex injected "Then let's do it! Let's get me back in that body!" "Because I don't know how to" said Joanne raising her voice "Just because someone goes over Niagara Falls and lives doesn't mean the next person can." Alex crossed his arms in anger over this answer and glared at Joanne as she said, "Both times I did it I was in a top of the line hospital with highly trained nurses and doctors just seconds away."

"Take me up there, I have to give it a shot" said Alex with a gusto to his voice that seemed to please Nathan and upset Joanne as she said, "Ok, I'll explain a few things. When it happened to me I was with people that could handle it and if I had a watch on my wrist right now it would say 6:14 which means your body has been without oxygen for nineteen minutes. You probably know what that means to your brain." Cutting her off Alex said "Oh yeah, I've read stories of people that have gone thirty minutes or more and have been fine." "Those are just extremely rare occurrences", said Nathan "the rule of thumb is about twenty-five minutes give or take, and then it's pretty much over." "So we've got time to do this" said Alex with his voice still crackling with enthusiasm. It was the type that Joanne was dreading to steal from him with what she perceived to be the truth of the situation and said "Because getting you up there is the easy part, you can't just 'get in' like it's a car."

Not particularly liking this answer Alex turned his attention to Nathan and asked, "What about that one woman you told me about?"

"Meredith?" asked Nathan.

"Yeah Meredith! You said she kept jumping in and out somehow"

"Man I don't have a clue how that happened to her, it just did. I'll tell you this, my body was really broken. So badly so that I couldn't go back, but hers wasn't as bad, but just enough I guess."

"So what about my body, is it beyond repair?"

"I don't know that answer but I do know it's taken a beating and you're not in it" said Joanne wanting to cease Alex from entertaining any further notion of going back into his body as he once again protested her intentions by saying "You once said to 'Prove them wrong', you said it, I remember!" Seeing her own logic and motto turned against her Joanne tried to dampen the strategy of a rejuvenated Alex and said "That's not fair, what you are asking isn't fair. Not to you or us."

"How isn't it fair?" asked Alex crossing his arms proudly.

"Because it's like telling someone there is hope in a hopeless situation instead of preparing them for the truth"

"The truth is I have nothing left to lose and while I'm here it's worth a shot, I'll fight until the end"

"Why fight?" asked Nathan.

"Because of her, Samantha's a good enough reason. If I could go back it would be for her. For me as well, I'm a good enough reason."

The stress of the moment was now showing on the face of Joanne and she realized that as hard as she fought the notion to simply give up she still could not accept this idea in her heart. "This is big. You know you're asking a lot of us", she said looking at both Alex and Nathan while plotting her next move. "I don't even know where to start, it's like trying to tell someone how to be a painter or a poet, either the feeling is in you or it's not." The two men remained silent as she further went on to add "Then there's the problem of once we get up into that apartment and time picking up as normal." "What does that mean?" asked Alex having a good sense as to what the answer would be as Nathan chimed in "It means that things will happen really fast and we'll hit the twenty-five minute mark and when that happens, well things are well over at that point. Your body will have been without oxygen for quite a while and the damage is going to be just too much." "In other words" said Joanne "This is do or die."

"I just wish I knew how to make this happen" said Joanne staring up that the apartment on the second floor as Nathan caught her attention and said, "I think I have an idea." "Go on", said Joanne not sure what Nathan had in store to suggest but was willing at this point to at least listen. "We need to get a hold of Jacob, he might have some sort of clue, after all he was there when Meredith did it and when you got out and went back" he said as Joanne's eyes became wide and she shook her head and said "I don't know about that, do you even know where to find him or contact him?" "So this is that Jacob guy you've both mentioned before?" asked Alex "I've heard you talk about him." Nathan smiled as he began to explain to Alex about Jacob and said "Yeah Jacob has a job as a recruiter for our gig. When we started he would check in to make sure we were doing ok. Real good soul, no pun intended." "But he's all about the rules and if we have people looking for us then he'll try and talk us into giving him over" said Joanne being a realist as Alex spoke up and replied "You know I really don't care. If you think he may have some idea how to do this then I say let's do it."

The three gathered a bit closer and assembled a crude plan as Joanne said "Alright, since Alex is mine until they arrive then he's sticking with me" linking her arm through his as Nathan nodded and she added "Also Nathan, I take any and all responsibility for this, I just talked you into all of this, got it?" "Well you kind of did" he replied with a smile "But I'll tell them you were forceful and it scared me." Looking back at Nathan she said "You just do you best to get a hold of Jacob. I'll get him back up there to his body."

"Why not just hang out down here until they get back?" asked Alex.

"Because he may not be able to find Jacob and I at least want you trying. I don't want time to slip by and us just waiting for Nathan to show up."

With that being said all three shared a glance as Joanne spoke and simply said, "We'll let's give it a shot. Don't be long Nathan." "You don't worry about me, you just get him into that body" said Nathan punching Alex in the arm as he said "Good luck" and turned and sprinted away while looking upwards for what Alex could only hope were clues or signs as to where this Jacob person might be. "Listen to me Alex" she said making sure she had his attention "When I get you into that apartment things are going to seem overwhelming. You have to ignore it and try to concentrate on getting into the body. It may seem like building a house of cards during a tornado, but you have to try, is that clear?" "Oh perfectly" he said as the two turned to make their way towards the stairs leading up to the apartment. "Hey Joanne, just one more thing" said Alex.

"What's that?"

"Can you tell I'm really scared?"

Joanne stopped short of the first aged metal step and turned towards Alex and said "It's okay to be scared, sometimes fear is the best way we can really tell we care about ourselves and others. But let's get up there." And with that answer she grabbed his hand and the two began their assent.

CHAPTER 17

Joanne and Alex made the brief climb to the top of the stairs and Alex noticed how the usual metallic clanking noise that he had grown accustomed to hearing under his feet was absent and this too was another subtle reminder of his dire situation. The weather beaten maroon door now stood in the way of the two and Alex thought about how it was a strange separation from this brief existence with Joanne and Nathan and the chaos he knew and carelessly lived. "Just remember what we talked about" said Joanne "You have to focus and it's going to be hard, really hard, but you have to." "You got it" was the response put forth by Alex as he became panic-stricken and placed his hand on his chest and said, "We have a problem."

"What's the problem?" asked a concerned Joanne.

"The feeling from earlier."

"In your chest?

"Yeah. It's not there. It's gone."

"That certainly is a problem", said Joanne with her hand out stretched and ready to push on the door and then without warning it suddenly flew inward exposing the inside of the apartment. There stood Robbie staring back at Alex with a look of angst and guilt as his eyes spoke more than his mouth every could about the strain on his mind. With his focus so intense that his eye lids seem to flex and revealed the tiny muscles underneath. His recent experiences told him he had nothing to fear from this man anymore, still he flinched in his presence and felt intimidated as if he were a bug under his shoe. The dirty and torn flannel shirt he had worn earlier in the day was still on his body, the dingy jeans and black shoes as well. At this moment Alex was a deer in the headlights to Robbie and even Joanne had trouble shaking him loose from this power Robbie had over him. He felt a steady shaking on his left side as Alex lost track of how long he stood in front of the apartment entry. "Hurry up, he's in here!" was all Robbie said as the certain feeling that Alex had experienced earlier came over him as he realized that two paramedics had been coming up the stairs and had passed through Alex with their gear and gurney.

This action once again threw Alex off of his balance and he caught himself on the edge of the door not completely falling to the floor and noticed Joanne stood unmoved. "Come on, we have work to do" she said trying to filter all emotion from her voice while helping him to his feet and putting her arm behind him to guide Alex past the door jamb. Although she didn't mean to sound the way she did he was reminded that this was a job for her and there was a task at hand. But it was when they both re-entered the apartment that the gravity of the situation made itself once again known with a more appreciable mood.

The site of Gina sitting on the couch weeping caught his attention and he couldn't help but take notice of how frail she seemed in this light as she held her head in her hands and cried. "In the back room, he's in the back" said Robbie to the two paramedic in their dark blue jackets and matching pants. "What's his name?" asked a paramedic as Robbie said "Alex, it's Alex." "Sir you need to stay here, we'll take it from this point on" as he put up his hand to stop Robbie from following them. This however did nothing to prevent Alex and Joanne from tracing his steps from what seemed like an eternity but in reality was only a mere nineteen minutes ago.

For some reason the apartment seemed even messier than it had before, the scuff and claw marks on the walls, the soiled carpet, this ill kept place that matched its occupant seemed to warn those who dared to enter. Warnings that both Alex and Reno couldn't seem to see at the time and to which Gina was just beginning to wise up to. Alex was surprised at how much he was shaking as Joanne held his hand and pulled him to follow the paramedics down the hallway and into the small and cluttered bedroom and he could only rationalize this by telling himself he had too much fear inside of him. The type of fear that could have kept him alive if he had not fooled himself into thinking that he was immortal and immune from the results of his careless actions. Before he could reflect any longer he felt Joanne give a final pull and he realized he was now in the small bedroom and standing over his lifeless body.

Both eyes were slightly open and looking towards the ceiling with his pupils as wide and dark as a moonless night. His skin was more pail than what he had remembered and noticed it had a washed out quality.

His mouth too was open and Alex noticed the three cavities that he had repaired several years ago and remembered the pain involved. He used the excuse to call into work the following day as he just watched cartoons and ate ice cream all afternoon and loved how it took him back to a simpler version of himself. The version he wished he could always be before the pressures of life warped his view of the world and instead of making him stronger only made his weaker.

The sound of a case of medical devices opening shook Alex from the trance he briefly found himself in as the two men began their work on what all in the room must have considered a lost cause. "I'm getting tired of these sort of runs," said the man sporting gray hair and a mustache with the nametag that read 'John' "Why do people do things like this?" as he checked for a pulse. The other man readied a syringe into a small vile and pulled fluid into its body and asked, "Have a pulse?"

"No. Nothing. He's a cold one", replied Mark.

Hearing this the man removed the needled form the small vile and stored it back into his case as the other took a small flashlight and began examining the hollow eyes of the body and after his inspection said "Yeah, I'm calling this one, we're just too late." After his announcement Joanne shook Alex and said, "You need to get in there and now! What are you waiting for? Now!" But the site of the two men working on his body and hearing their proclamation of his end seemed to be too much for Alex and he lost what little focus and determination he had from moments earlier and said "I just don't know what to do! I can't!" and quickly exited the room in shame.

Returning the to the living room Alex and Joanne found two police officers questioning a highly defensive Robbie while paying little attention to a shocked and grief stricken Gina just several feet away that was now crying even louder than before. "So you're 'friend' just dropped dead while you were out?" asked the first officer with his blond hair poking out from under his police cap. "Like I said, he's not my friend, but more like a friend of a friend" replied Robbie "All I know is the guy had a drug problem, real fucked up type. He probably shot up before he got here, I don't know because I stepped out." The second officer said nothing but instead looked around the small apartment and took notes on his small pad of paper and silently assessed Robbie and Gina.

"Come on, let's take this outside" said one officer with

the blonde hair, "I can't hear myself think, we'll talk to her in a second when she calms down."

Robbie's eyes shifted back and forth sizing up the two officers and anticipating their line of questions as he replied "Sure. Sure let's do that officers" as he flashed a smile that seemed to say he wasn't going to succumb to the interrogation they had in mind.

The fascination of the group was short lived as Joanne pulled on the arm of Alex and asked, "Alex! What happened in there? I told you it was going to be tough but you froze up on the both of us." Alex looked to the floor in shame and knew deep down why he couldn't concentrate and why he couldn't complete the task at hand. The embarrassment was too great to speak of and the continued crying of Gina only compounded the issue, but more importantly brought it into the light.

"I'll tell you why," said a familiar voice that caught Joanne's attention as she swung around to face the door to discover Nathan that had returned with Jacob. His eyes were a grayish blue that seemed to be able to see right through a person or a situation for what it really was and his hair was as white and wavy. A simple black cardigan over a blue t-shirt and light gray pants were all that adorned this man that Joanne held in such high esteem as his outfit hardly seemed to fit his role or position. Still he needed no introduction as he strolled towards Alex and Joanne with Nathan right behind him.

"This boy is scared", said Jacob "Scared to his core. Scared so much so that it's clouding his better judgment. With your better judgment clouded you do stupid things like what we see here." There was almost an afterglow to his statement that was short lived as Joanne exclaimed, "Wow, so you found us?" "Well talk later after we figure this guy out", said Jacob pointing at Alex as he added with a small laugh "She really went out on a limb for you." "Yeah I know, I'm so sorry. I don't think this should go on her record, she was only looking out for me, you know, just trying to help" said Alex trying to defend Joanne in the best and simplest manner he could. With his grandfatherly eyes looking on, Jacob said with a smile "Well like I said we'll talk but it's hard to fault someone with the 'never say die' attitude, forgive the pun. I just wish more people had it."

Alex felt some relief in this statement but not for himself, rather in the notion that Joanne could emerge from this with little or even no disciplinary action against her. The sight of the two officers questioning

Robbie outside the door caught the attention of Alex and seeing this Jacob snapped his fingers to regain the young man's attention and said "You pay too much attention to that train wreck of a man out there, he's got his own problems to sort out and you've let him pollute you." "I know," replied Alex in a voice that could best be described as 'mousy' and steeped in embarrassment "I didn't mean for it to be that way." "Well that's a moot point now and we have other matters to discuss. I know you have toyed around with wanting to go back otherwise you wouldn't be here. I know how it works, that longing to go back, to get back in" said Jacob in a voice that made Alex feel at home even in this place and time. He continued with "Now either I can tell you why you are so scared, or you can tell me. I honestly think it's better for you to tell me, you know that old adage about confession and such." Joanne stood by feeling more nervous than she let on, but taking mental notes as to how Jacob was handling the situation.

Alex rubbed his mouth and looked at the floor and said with a sigh, "Yeah, I'm real scared, that's the truth." The body language that Jacob demonstrated to Alex was clear and helped to further put him at ease, the skinny gray haired man stood with his hands clasped behind his back and flashed a slight smile as Alex said "Going back sounds nice and honestly I would only go back for one reason. But." The sudden end to his statement made Jacob raise one eyebrow and ask "But what? Surely this reason must be worthwhile? Worth all of this running?" "Oh she is!" said Alex with an energy to his voice that was missing earlier as Jacob turned to Joanne and said "Ah, so this reason is a girl, now that makes more sense." "A real cute one too, total class act" said Nathan as all looked his way shocked at his observation as he said in his defense "You know I'm right."

"Going back for a 'girl' can be dangerous you know, after all people can change, things can change. Nothing is guaranteed out there", said Jacob, his words settled down on the room and did little to lift the spirits of those that could hear it. "I know that", replied Alex "But she's different" Turning towards Joanne Jacob then said "And the picture becomes more clear when he exposes himself and his motivations." Turning back towards Alex the look in the eyes of Jacob were more piercing as he said "But there is more than love, we could talk about that all day, we need to get back to the fear" This put Alex on edge and it showed in his voice as he said "Yeah I'll tell you why the fear is there. I let her down twice. Once by being some sort of junkie and then by, well I guess dying today. What if I go back and I can't keep it together and I do it all over again, then I've done nothing but hurt her again." Jacob nodded his head and said "Indeed what if. What if all of that? You understand what I said earlier that nothing is guaranteed. I like that you know of the dangers in false promises. So many people promise things so lightly as if on a whim. I can tell you how Joanne went back."

"How?" asked Alex.

"Her motivation was strong and she knew she would not stop fighting until the very end. That's a good motto for one's life."

"Well now I agree, a little late but I agree"

"But she also understood the risks and how her body was in the shape it was in, this too went into her decision to go back and then to leave."

The conversation somehow managed to continue over the constant crying of Gina on the couch as all were interrupted by the sound of a buzzing phone on vibrate. The four gathered in the middle of the room all turned towards the unsuspecting woman as they watched her search her coat pockets until she found her phone and looked at it. The vibration stopped but no call had been received nor had a call been recorded. Gina wiped her eyes and settled herself as she did not want to sound

like a mess if and when a call did make it through. She
held her phone in her hands as she put her head down
and thought about the way the afternoon had unfolded
and in turn the past several years of her life. Quietly she
wondered what an existence far from here might be
like. What she might be doing for a living or if we were
all slaves to patterns and situations that were the
makings of fate, and if it was all just beyond our control.

Nathan took the most pity on her and only wished he
could help in some way to straighten out or guide this
woman's life only to have his thoughts interrupted by
the sound of the buzzing that had returned as Gina
could then sense it by her feet as Nathan took several
steps towards her for a closer look. She reached down
and discovered a phone that was not hers under the
couch and felt it twitch in her hand as each movement
seemed as if the phone were throwing a fit much like a
child would for attention. The little screen left no
mystery of who was calling as it read 'Samantha' and
Gina knew this person only from how Alex spoke of her
often and in the highest regard.

Unknown to her Gina had an audience paying close
attention as Alex muttered, "That's my phone" but still
had no idea of who would be calling. Accepting the call
she slowly raised the phone to her ear and in a quiet

and shaky voice asked "Hello?" On the other end of the call was Samantha sitting with her back to the passenger side window in Elise's car as she said "Hi. I'm trying to get a hold of Alex. This should be his phone, I really need to speak to him." At this request Gina felt the urge to stall even though she could not derail the inevitable task of delivering the horrible news. "Oh this must be Samantha, Alex always says such great things about you" said Gina with a quiver to her voice that sent a wave of dread through the girl on the other end, but before she could react Gina said "It's nice to finally hear your voice, I'm his friend Gina." Hearing Gina say this Alex felt panic once again sweep through his being as he said, "No, no this can't happen like this, please stop this!" Samantha was more than sensing that something was not right as she demanded to speak with Alex in a way that was more direct and stern.

Samantha put her head down as she then felt the hand of Elise on her back as she said "Put Alex on, just put Alex on the phone please" as the silence between the two woman settled into the valley of the conversation and Gina began to cry again and said "I wish I could but I can't" Hearing this Samantha also began to weep and asked "Why?" now realizing what a sad and strange question to ask and knowing there was no reason to inquire other than a natural reaction that people seem have in an attempt to avoid the tragically obvious truth. In part of her mind she knew that she was piecing her emotions and intuitions together throughout the day as Gina played spoiler to the tension and said "Because. I don't know how to say this but he's dead." Through the phone's speaker Gina could hear the sound of a person's life being broken, no words were spoken but the audible crying communicated enough to Gina to take a silent and personal vow to never associate with the likes of Robbie or his chemical pursuits ever again. Hearing this Samantha felt powerless to everything around her and although she wanted to know where he was and what happened she lacked the strength to pursue further questions as she collapsed and slumped over.

The sobbing was cut short by Samantha ending the call leaving Gina in silence and with the promise she had made to herself with the phone still against her ear. Not knowing the call had ended Alex walked towards Gina and he began shouting into the phone "Samantha I'm still here! I'm coming back and I'll change! I promise!" but with the phone slipping away from her face and closing told Alex the conversation had concluded. He dropped to his knees kneeling beside the couch next to Gina that had once again started crying and every so often saying small prayers and asking for guidance. This was a side that she kept to herself as she had long since felt separated from her religious upbringing, but still her prayers went out "Please help me" was the plea she kept in constant rotation. Still Alex felt he lacked the strength or will to stand and face the other three that could detect his presences. He listened to the quiet prayers whispered from Gina and knew he lacked an anchor in his life. It was much in the same way she did and was somewhat curious to the jealousy he felt that she had religion or some sort of beliefs to fall back on in a time of need. His safety net was Samantha and he was the one that failed her.

Turning himself around and sitting on the ground Alex drew his knees to his chest and rested his head on them, to him this was the lowest of the lows and the most concentrated dose of defeat he could ever imagine and with that he too simply began to cry. The sensation felt alien to him since he had not allowed himself this emotional outlet in years and really longer than he could recall as he struggled to remain still so he could simply just recall. To remember all that had been, the way he felt his childhood was as normal as it could have been or how he missed his parents that he had grown distant for for no good reason. He thought deeply about Stan and how he was blessed to know this person and how he was someone that always gave Alex great memories and a lot to think about even after his passing.

And mostly he thought about Samantha and wondered

how she would be altered by this and just wanted her to be okay even though his instincts were telling him otherwise. And this only fueled more tears from the corners of his eyes. Alex looked up and took note of Jacob, Nathan, and Joanne in the middle of the room. Nathan had his arms crossed and starred at the ground with the stance of a humbled giant, Joanne looked distraught with one arm hanging at her side and the other raised to behind her head as her right hand held a section of bunched up hair and he could tell she had a hard time making eye contact with anyone in the room. Lastly there was Jacob that stood in the middle with his arms again behind his back with his head slightly turned and showing a slight smile.

It was the sly type of smile that says 'I know something that you don't know' as the two men remained locked in a stare for a brief moment until Jacob said "Joanne. Nathan. You two need to pay attention because this is important." As they returned to focusing their attention back on the current situation, but still both stayed silent as Jacob continued by asking "Now you see what's going on here, what's out of the ordinary?" "He's crying," said Joanne looking down on Alex as he too was surprised by this action. "That's right! He's crying. That's a very big deal because it's either a physical manifestation of his thoughts and feelings in an overwhelmed state. Or it's because he's truly sorry for what's happened and wants to go back in the worst possible way. Or both. It would be an understatement to call it rare in this line of work. But it can happen and it means he's learned something after all."

Hearing this Alex just nodded his head as he watched Jacob take a few steps closer and crouch down in front of Alex as he put his hand on his shoulder and said "Son you need to listen to me and listen good." Alex looked at Jacob and could now sense how much this older man was pulling for him but not making any guarantees as he said, "I need for you to understand something's of great importance." "What's that?" asked Alex. "Well for starters your body has been in a rather dead state for quite a while and going back now is very risky, I would hate to see you have brain damage from this." The statement was something that had been expressed to him before but now Alex took it with a little more seriousness and asked "Ok, what else?" "And on top of that you still have that junk in your system, you would have to deal with it and it's an uphill fight. Trust me I was a smoker at one point so I understand what an addiction is. And then there is paying for the laws you've broken with an illegal substance. The cops outside just won't look the other way."

Jacob stood up over Alex and looked down as Alex fought to pull himself together and pondered the issues and obstacles laid forth by Jacob. "Now I guess the point of knowing all of this is if you can give me a good reason why you need one more shot. Even after knowing the risk, just one good heart-felt reason." Alex wiped his eyes and stared up at the man looking down and simply said "Two reasons, me and Samantha." As the two remained locked in a stare Jacob said "You seem pretty sure about that" to which Alex replied "I've never been so sure of anything in my life. No pun intended."

Jacob reached out his hand as Alex accepted and could feel this older looking man easily pull him to his feet as he said, "Then we have work to do." As Alex listened to Jacob he was not sure quite what to make of his statement or how we would pull off what seemed like the impossible as Jacob turned to Nathan and pointed to Gina and said "Nathan, I need for you to stay with her, she's going to need some guidance to get out of this. You can think of it as training for future advancement, plus you've been on the other end of these kind of scenes before so you know what should and shouldn't be said." "You got it" was the proud reply from Nathan as he then stood almost sentry by Gina as she doubled over and rolled onto the floor facing the couch and the scattered debris underneath. She noticed the crumpled up fast food wrappers and rolls of dog hair under the couch with a thick layer of dust, but one thing that caught her attention was a small plastic bag

CHAPTER 18

Alex and Joanne walked side by side and Jacob stayed close behind as the three made their way down the hall to the bedroom and Alex was further bothered by what he then saw. The paramedics had already gotten him onto the gurney and secured in a black body bag, the two men were swift and silent in their duties and completed the task without even alerting those in the living room of their activities. The paramedic John closed the case and he asked the other "Can we clear that corner? I don't feel like taking this guy off of here. It's bad enough he weighs more than he looks and smells like he hasn't had a shower in a while." "Yeah" replied the other "It'll be tight but we can do it, and have a little respect. I hope you smell this good when you die" as he added a small laugh. Under the plastic they could clearly see the outline and form of Alex as Jacob said "Really you should take better care of yourself and it starts with self-respect and a shower." Alex nodded as Joanne interrupted and asked "Well now what?"

Jacob smiled and turned towards Joanne to say, "Well he is yours to guide so you need to do what seems natural, think about how you did it and how you got back in." Joanne grabbed Alex by both arms to force his attention away from the scene of his covered body then looked him square in the eyes and said, "Ok, this is it and you know the risks." "Yeah I sure do", said Alex stretching and then clenching his fingers as Jacob interjected "One other thing Alex. You more than likely won't remember any of this but sometimes people do from time to time recall bits and fragments so just do your best to remember."

Feeling a new surge of empowerment Joanne addressed Alex and said "Well this is it so to quote my mom 'get in there and fight' and if you do get back don't stop ever. Keep going like you have a damn good reason because you do." Joanne then raised her hand again to place over the face of Alex and to anticipate this he closed his eyes and felt the soft palm of her hand over his eyelids. He thought long and hard about what paths he had been down not just recently but within the past ten years of his life and even longer. The people he had met and kept company with, co-workers he both got along with and had skirmishes with over the pettiest of subjects and was embarrassed of these small but important actions woven into the fabric of his life.

From his parents and past friends and the distance that now seemed to exist between him and others that simply should not be. But more over his thoughts were focused on Samantha. He loved how she could take a bad situation and plan a way out, or a simple evening and make it stay on his mind until this very day. It wasn't so much her physical being that always caught and held his attention but rather the entire person. The voice and laughter that would always settle down over him like a warm blanket on an autumn evening, or text messages that would arrive at three in the morning for him to read when he awoke. He always knew Samantha was a person that knew the small things did matter and always added up to the larger sum in life.

An unsettling feeling suddenly hit Alex as the experience was different this time from what it had been and the past. The wind that he had grown accustomed to was all but absent, gone too was the feeling of comfort that was always hung in the air, and the last feeling to leave was the warmth of the palm Joanne. Opening his eyes the first thing Alex saw was black, everywhere nothing but deep unmistakable black. It was the environment that one might be subject to in a deep cave devoid of light. "Joanne! Joanne! Where are you?" he screamed as loud as he could "It's not working! Something is wrong!" Then came the taste in his mouth, it was a tinny flavor that made his tongue recoil in disgust and made him choke. It was only when he couldn't see his extremities that he became even more worried as Alex tried to put his hands to his face but they felt as though they were either weights and impossible to move or perhaps just gone all together.

The gurney hit the wall with a great amount of force as Mark said "Hey careful man, he's not in any hurry so let's take it easy" as they tried to maneuver it into the hallway. John looked down as he pondered turning the gurney sideways and decided to strap the body of Alex down in order to turn the platform on its side just slightly. "Hold up" he said "Let's tie him down in case we decide to turn this at an angle, I don't feel like picking him up if he drops". With one man on each end of the gurney they released cargo straps from underneath the front and rear of the metal structure and Mark was the first to completely securing the legs of Alex and looked to see the job John was doing and thought how strange it was that the person that lived in this apartment had the air-conditioner on in April and at maximum rate. That would be the only explanation as to why the black plastic covering the body was moving by the right hip of the person underneath. But it was also odd that no other part of the material was being jostled by the air from the vents. Mark looked up and inspected the ceiling and noticed that there weren't any vents located in this part of the apartment and said, "John, stop moving. Do you seen any place air could be getting in here?" John complied and ceased in his attempt to strap Alex down and joined Mark in his search for an air source.

John did his brief scan of the ceiling and even the floor before looking at Mark and asking "Okay, you got me, what's the point?" Then he noticed the expression of wonder on the face of Mark as he in turn pointed to the spot of plastic that began as a slow rise and fall but had now become a rapid twitching motion that left both men now perplexed. "No way" said John wide eyed as Mark replied, "You don't think?" Mark unzipped the bag revealing the frantic hand of Alex moving by his side as though it were a separate being yearning to break free from the rest of the body. "Oh fuck!" said John "I think we've got a live one!"

The shaking that began in his right hand quickly traveled up his arm and then into the rest of his body until his whole physical being shook violently as if Alex were racked by convulsions. This sent Mark and John into action still not sure if they should trust what they thought they were seeing happen before them as John began calling out orders. He starting with "See if you have a pulse or anything, I'll get check the dilation. Alex turned his head to the side and his body convulsed expelling a large amount of mucus that had gathered in his lungs before and after his passing. The pressure exerted by his chest to free his blocked airways was only then exceeded by the movement of his lungs pulling in air. Alex noticed it felt fresh and new in a way he had forgotten a breath of air could smell and even taste.

Alex quickly sat straight up to see a shocked man at the foot of the gurney as he continued gasping for air as if a man saved from drowning. "Holy crap" was all the man at his feet could say before Alex felt and arm around the his chest as he was forced back onto the mattress as he stared up at the poorly spackled ceiling before being blinded by a light shining into his eyes. It was pure and white in its intensity as he heard a voice asking "Sir! Can you tell me your name? Do you know where you are?" As his pupils darted back and forth he replied "Alex. I'm Alex" as a hand slid up his shirt and he felt the cold circular metal from a stethoscope on his chest. He made another attempt to sit up as Alex realized he lacked the strength to rise again and was being held down as Mark said "Alex buddy you have to work with me so don't fight, I have to get your vitals, do you understand?" This request of Alex was all but lost as he had one real thought and one real concern.

"Samantha" he said in what barely registered as a response "I have to call Samantha; she needs to know."

"I have his signs, we can move him now" said Mark as Alex saw the bright light disappear leaving spots as Mark and John wrestled with the stubborn gurney a little more force as it gouged holes into the drywall and scuffed the paint into an even worse state. Alex could feel the two struggle as the only part to remain in place were his feet which were still securely strapped down. His focus was once again on the ceiling as Alex noticed the dim light fixture pass overhead and knew he was now entering into the living area and could hear the gasp of Gina as she said "Oh my God!" and out on the small porch area beyond the front door he could hear Robbie arguing with two men as they were all raising their voices to each other in a debate that had grown very heated. Alex could feel a strap goes across his chest as John said "Alex, I need for you to stay calm, we're going to be moving you down the stairs now and this will hold you in place, is that clear?" "Yes" was his response as he turned his head to see Gina rising up from the ground with a stunned wide-eyed look on her face.

Mark retrieved his radio and made a call "Jackson Park dispatch be expecting a white male mid to late twenties, possible overdoes with heart failure." This proclamation was reflected on the face of Gina as pure fear but all the same seemed less frightening to Alex due to his thoughts being on Samantha. He motioned Gina over to the side of the Gurney as the two listen to

Mark conclude his radio transmission to the hospital as he said "No he's still alive, ETA is about ten minutes." As she got within three feet of the gurney John put up his hands and said "I'm sorry lady he's got to get out of here now." Normally stressful situations would crumple the processing ability of Gina and reduce her to a bystander unable to deal with what was happening.

However, this time she felt what to her was an inner voice coaching her on what to say as she almost instinctively blurted out "But I have to go with him, you see I'm his sister!" "Is this true Alex?" asked Mark as Alex looked up at Gina and quietly nodded his head. Alex then felt the metal platform once again gain momentum as they made their way to the door leading outside and he found himself bathed in more fresh air and now sun light as Gina made sure to retrieve the green jacket from the side of the couch, the same green jacket that so many people associated with Alex.

Being in full view of both police officers was comforting to Alex until he found himself under the stare of Robbie that now had an look of elation on his face as he said "Alex buddy what did you do? Man you gave us a scare. See officers, he's ok there's not a problem here." Alex didn't have much time to reflect on this as he disappeared from site and he began the downward journey to the courtyard below and then the ambulance. Gina gave Robbie a long hard look with steely eyes and a squared jaw her teeth were clenched behind her red lips as she made sure not to lash out at this pathetic man. One of the officers followed and asked a few questions before being cut off by John as he said "Sir with all due respect we have to get this guy to Jackson pronto so no questions." The officer pulled on the arm of Gina and said "Wait a second we have some questions for you." Gina was confused and only wanted to accompany Alex to a better place as the same paramedic again spoke up and said, "You can ask questions as we load this guy up, she's his sister and she's going with us." The officer was clearly showing his rookie status as he said "I'm sorry ma'am I just need to know if you have anything to add to this, like a statement. Anything to wrap this up."

Gina looked at the officer and then to the top of the stairs where Robbie and the other officer were perched and still have a lively conversation that would rise and fall in intensity and all the while the grin he flashed never seemed to leave his face, the cockiness was undeniable even from down below. It was that sort of smile that a truly self-serving person would have, and knew she too was guilty of that expression several times in her life. But she had wised up over the years and even more over that past several hours. "Ma'am" said the officers regaining her attention. "Oh a statement" said Gina rubbing her cheek and leaning closer towards the officer as she added, "You need to look under his couch, in the living room. Please do that? Promise me?" Slowly backing away Gina did her best to communicate the urgency to this young man with the look in her eyes. In return his eyes rose up in unison as he said "Oh. I think I understand" to which Gina nodded and said "Just promise me. I need to go with my brother now" as she could hear the legs of the gurney fold under as they loaded Alex into the orange and white ambulance. Mark was in the back of the truck to see to Alex as John assisted Gina up and into the double doors before closing them as she stared back at the young officer as she mouthed the word "Please" and he in return nodded his head in reassurance.

The engine of the truck was turned on and she saw and heard the officer smack the double doors indicating that they are secured to begin the trip to the hospital. In the small amount of time that Gina had taken her attention away from Alex she was surprised at how much work the paramedic had done. He already had an oxygen mask on him as he started cutting away the black t-shirt that Alex wore revealing the dog tags that he always kept close. Seeing this Mark decided to make conversation with Alex as he asked "Oh military huh? What branch? I was Air Force myself." Leaning in knowing Alex was in no condition to answer back Mark noticed the name did not match up with Alex as he said

"Well whoever you are these have to come off" and gave a lateral rip as he broke the small metal chain that made the weak Alex attempt to sit up once again as Gina said "Those belonged to a friend, I'll make sure it's safe for him" as Mark handed the tags to Gina.

Mark was still working his craft on Alex but all really seemed a blur as a few lines did seem to make it to the patient. He was able to understand such statements as "Alex you seemed to have stepped out for a few minutes" and "You should have some stories after this one" but really little mattered to him at that point except one thing. He continued his stare at Gina and smiled knowing she was leaving that terrible apartment with him and did his best to communicate what he really needed to say. Under the plastic mask that covered his mouth she thought she could see him saying "Samantha" over and over again as Gina reached into her purse and produced the familiar cell phone of Alex as he nodded with approval. Gina activated the phone and scrolled through recent calls and came to Samantha and then dialed. Not really sure what to say Gina thought for a second about how it would feel to receive such horrible news as her pondering was cut short by a serious "Hello" on the other end.

Gina did not recognize this voice and feared she had the

wrong number as she said, "Hi, I need to speak with Samantha." The woman on the other end of the line said "This is Elise, I'm her friend. Is this Gina?" "Yeah it is", she said as Elise could hear the sirens on the background and wondered while they were using the sirens for a person that had died. Elise looked over had her friend that was a destroyed mess practically on the floor of the car and said "Gina I know you can understand when I say this but she is in no shape to talk. Just tell us where they are taking him." Now in turn Gina could hear Samantha crying and said, "Well that's just it. He's not dead anymore." "Excuse me?" asked Elise in disbelief "You had better not be fucking with her because that's sick." "Oh no I'm not, we're on the way to the hospital right now, Jackson Park" said Gina only to be cut off by Elise saying "Hold on." Gina could hear Elise comforting Samantha that at times couldn't control her grief as she said "Samantha! Sam honey, you need to take this call. I don't understand but you need to talk to her!"

"Hello" was the next thing Gina heard from Samantha that had trouble even producing this simple everyday greeting. Gina could hear the way she was shocked and had trouble breathing as she said "Samantha this is Gina."

"I know" she replied broken.

"I really don't know how to explain this, but he's not dead."

"What?"

"I'm in the ambulance with him now and he's alert and breathing, I can't explain it"

"This-What?" stammered Samantha.

"He's been asking for you. We're on our way to Jackson Park Hospital right now."

"I need to speak to him now!"

"He has a mask on. For breathing, but I'll hold the phone to his ear" as Gina then leaned forward and with Mark's permission put the phone to the ear of Alex.

"Alex honey don't die, I'm on my way and I'll be there soon!" His senses seemed overloaded and yet he felt numb all at the same time and blamed this on the drugs that were still coursing through his veins and felt angry that they were a barrier between him and the rest of the world. But more importantly between him and Samantha. He listened to her express how much she loved him and knew his longing to change was not guaranteed. That his previous promises were shallow and never panned out, however this time he knew he could not fail.

Since Mark had stabilized Alex he quietly offered to hold the phone for Gina so she could sit back in the small jump seat beside him and wear the seat belt as she could feel every turn the truck made through traffic. The jacket of Alex felt reassuring in her hands as she held it tight and watched him listen to the phone call with two simple tear lines trailing down his face and into his hair. Watching this made her clutch the jacket even harder as she noticed the outline of a square object in the chest pocket and fought the urge to go through his property as she did respect his privacy.

This however was a losing cause as she simply could not fight the curiosity any longer as her hand dove in to the green jacket to solve the mystery. The object was cool and smooth like paper, but even more so on the ends where it became metallic in nature. Pulling the object into the daylight Gina felt oddly foolish as to why Alex had a candy bar in his possession. This was something she simply did not expect although she found it to be a pleasant surprise as it offered solace to better thoughts and memories. Ones that she had lost track of and desperately needed to regain her connection with, the simpler things. Gina had her concentration clearly on the candy bar as Alex looked up while still listening to Samantha and tried to piece together in his mind why that particular candy bar seemed to have more meaning than a wrapped chocolate bar. This was cut short as Alex felt his attention needed to be back on Samantha as he began anticipating the seconds until he could see her again and hopefully start from a better place.

The End